ARCTIC BLOOD

A THRILLER

By James Raven

<u>Published through</u>

<u>Global House Publishing</u>

<u>http://www.james-raven.com/</u>

By the same author

Rollover

Urban Myth

Stark Warning

Brutal Revenge

After the Execution

Red Blitz

To mum and dad with love

ONE

I took the Norseman down to seven hundred feet above the sea and headed her into the gaping mouth of the fjord. Soon I was swallowed by the shadows of the mountains which rose sheer and grey with great white spires that gleamed in the sunlight.

There was no wind. Below, the ice-flecked water was as calm and blue as the sky overhead. The little town of Tasiilaq appeared beyond the first headland on a rocky shore that slopes into a small natural harbour.

It isn't much of a place by any standards, nothing more than a cluster of small wooden buildings housing a population of just over two thousand. Even so, it's by far the largest settlement on the east coast of Greenland. Situated some sixty miles below the Arctic Circle, it was at one time one of the most isolated communities in the world. Then they plonked an airfield on the nearby island of Kulusuk which opened up the east coast to outsiders. Before that only specially strengthened ships could get through and then only at the height of summer when the pack-ice melted.

A less favourable position for a town would be difficult to imagine. On one side is the Denmark Strait, that wide choppy stretch of sea between Greenland and Iceland that carries the Arctic ice on its great journey south during spring and summer. On the other side are the famous Icy Mountains, beyond which lie the desolate wastes of the Greenland Ice Cap.

I banked the Norseman in a wide circle and nosed her in towards the harbour. As far as I could tell it was almost completely ice-free, which is unusual even in July. There were two ships anchored down there, a handful of fishing boats, and Bill Osborn's Otter Amphibian, which was tied to the small wooden jetty.

The little town grew out of the bare grey rock on which it was spread and above it in the still morning air the red Danish flag hung limp from a white pole. All the houses were of the same matchbox design and painted in bright reds, blues and yellows.

The harbour came up to meet me. . . Three hundred feet . . . two hundred. . . a hundred. The floats hit the water and slid for about a hundred and fifty yards across the surface like two half-submerged torpedoes before finally coming to a halt. I brought the tail round and took her in towards the end of the low jetty.

A typical Greenland reception committee had already gathered consisting of a dozen or so gaily dressed Inuit kids and half as many adults who didn't look much taller. There were dogs around, barking like mad and generally making a nuisance of themselves. I glanced at my watch. It was still only eight which meant I'd made pretty good time.

I ran the Norseman up beside the jetty and saw Else Jensen in the crowd, his head and shoulders towering above the others. I killed the engine, unstrapped myself and pushed open the side door. I threw the mooring line to Jensen and he promptly secured it.

As I stepped down onto the jetty the kids started crowding me like I was some sort of celebrity. There were also those infamous Greenland dogs to contend with. I counted five in all — each living up to its reputation as being of an unfriendly disposition by baring its sharp teeth and snapping at my ankles.

Jensen came to the rescue by shouting and waving his arms at them. The dogs and kids scuttled off in every direction, leaving me standing alone, trying to look unruffled by the experience.

We both laughed and shook hands. His hand, like the rest of him, was big and it closed around mine like a steel claw.

"How are you?" I said.

"Fine, my friend. It is good to see you."

Jensen was a typical Dane: tall, broad shouldered, good looking. For three months now he'd been head of the construction gang working on the new school.

"You're early," he said.

"You can thank the weather. There wasn't a cloud all the way across the Strait."

It had taken me just under two hours to fly from my base in Iceland. For four years I'd been piloting charter flights out of the capital Reykjavik and the crossing to Greenland was a trip I made on a regular basis.

Jensen's pale blue eyes gestured towards the seaplane. "What have you got for us then?"

"Exactly what you ordered," I said. "Fifteen sacks of cement, various provisions, and those spare parts you've been in such a flap about."

"Good. I'll tell the guys to start unloading them. Are you going straight back?"

"After breakfast. Care to join me?"

"No time. I've got work to do."

I glanced out across the harbour which was dominated by a large grey ship.

"It's getting crowded around here," I said.

"That big bastard is Russian," Jensen said. "The oceanographic survey ship Lamanov. Arrived a few days ago."

The ship was anchored next to a Danish cargo vessel. There was a lot of bulky equipment on top. I picked out two cranes, a small submersible suspended from an arched beam, and an empty helipad.

In recent years the Russians had made themselves more conspicuous all over the Arctic and it was causing concern among other nations. The Kremlin had made no secret of the fact that it wanted the Arctic to become its main source of oil and gas as global warming melted the ice and gave access to untapped energy resources. It even had plans to establish a special military force in the region to 'protect its interests.'

Jensen got my attention by touching my arm.

"I think you're about to be propositioned, John," he said.

I followed his gaze. A man and a woman were walking towards us along the jetty.

"They're strangers in town, but they've been here for a couple of days," Jensen said. "They've been asking around this morning about getting a lift up north. I get the impression they're in a hurry."

They were both wearing expensive looking ski coats. His was grey and hers was orange. She was slim and about five six. He was tall, stocky and somewhere in his forties.

The woman beamed a smile at me as they approached. It was a pleasant smile. She had nice white teeth.

"Hi there," she said, with just the trace of an accent. "You must be John Preston."

I smiled back.

"I'm afraid so," I said. "And who might you be?"

"My name is Gudren Bragason. I'm very pleased to meet you."

She removed her glove and held out her hand for me to shake.

Her features were soft and freckled and she had a small pointed nose. Her hair was dark brown and matched the colour of her eyes. She wore it loose around her shoulders.

"This is my colleague, Viktor Sidorov," she said, waving a hand at her companion.

He had a heavy jowl and close-set eyes. His hair was cropped which made him look hard. I rolled his name around in my head. Sidorov. Had to be Russian.

He stepped forward to shake my hand. His grip was firm and assertive.

"It's good to meet you, Mr Preston," he said. "I watched you touch down just now. Very impressive."

"Years of practice," I said.

"Even so, bringing down an aircraft in these waters must entail significant risk. I imagine there's a lot of ice just below the surface."

I shrugged. "Most of it you can spot from the air. Plus the floats I've fitted are pretty sturdy."

"I'm sure they would have to be."

Jensen tapped my arm again. "I'll leave you to it, John. I'll get our stuff off the plane and maybe we'll catch up later."

"Sure thing," I said.

When he was out of earshot, Gudren said, "I hope you don't mind being accosted like this, Mr Preston. It's just that we're hoping very much that you can help us."

I arched my brow at her. "How so?"

She cleared her throat. "We're desperate to hire the services of a pilot to take us on a short trip. Believe it or not there are absolutely no float planes or helicopters here right now that are available for hire. As you know there's a shuttle helicopter to and from Kulusuk airport, but we can't use that."

I gestured towards Bill Osborn's Otter further along the jetty.

"Have you talked to the guy who owns that one?"

"You mean Mr Osborn?"

"That's right."

She nodded. "We actually made arrangements with him last night to take us up first thing this morning. We even gave him a deposit. Unfortunately he spent the money and is now in bed nursing a serious hangover."

"He makes a habit of it," I said.

Like me Bill Osborn was from England and as a freelance pilot had ventured far from home in search of an elusive fortune. In the process he had become an alcoholic. He was about my age, which was thirty-five, but unlike me he'd never settled in to the way of life here.

Bill's charter operation was also based in Reykjavik, which made him one of my main competitors. But there was always plenty of work around for small one-man operations. We were more versatile than the big companies. In summer we used the floats on our aircraft and in winter we swapped them for hydraulic skis. It meant we could land on the varied Arctic terrains all year round.

"We couldn't believe our luck when we saw you fly in," Gudren said. "The hotel receptionist told us who you were and we came right over."

"So where is it you want to go and when do you want to go?" I said.

"Do you know Mikkelson Island?" she asked.

I nodded. "North along the coast about a hundred miles. There's an old weather station there that's used these days for scientific research." I knew the place because I'd taken a party of Swedish geologists there the previous summer.

"We need to go there as soon as possible, Mr Preston. And because this is short notice we're prepared to pay you three times your normal rate."

"Really? Would it be a round trip?"

"No, we'll want you to take us on to Reykjavik if that's all right. We intend to spend only a very short time on the island."

I tried not to look too keen, but it wasn't easy because my plan was to go straight back anyway once I'd refuelled and had some breakfast. This job would be a bonus. How could I refuse?

"Is there anyone at the station right now?" I asked.

"A Norwegian geologist named Professor Peter Brun," Sidorov said. "Do you know him?"

"No, but I've heard of him."

Brun was an old timer who had studied the Greenland terrain for years and was as much a part of the country as the Humbolt Glacier. He worked as part of a small team monitoring and analysing the rate at which the ice cap was melting. There were others like him, all over the Arctic. An industry spawned by the great fear of global warming.

"I should explain that he's expecting us," Gudren said. "We contacted him earlier this morning by satellite phone and told him that we would be coming."

"So are you guys geologists too?" I asked.

"No we're not, Mr Preston," Gudren said. "We work for a company called Polar Holdings. It's an investment management company."

Now normally I don't pry into other people's business. I just take them where they want to go and don't ask questions unless I know they're happy to answer them. But this was an unusual request and their eagerness to get to such a remote island for some reason made me a little uneasy.

So I knotted my brow and said, "What makes you want to go to Mikkelson Island? It's the back of beyond. There's nothing there but the station and a tiny Inuit settlement."

Sidorov answered this time. He leaned towards me and said, "A man's body was recovered from the sea yesterday a mile out from the island, Mr Preston. It was taken to the station. Our reason for going there is to find out if the man was one of our colleagues."

*

I was glad I'd asked the question, even though the answer made my flesh tingle.

They wanted me to take them north to see a corpse. It was more than a little strange. Most customers wanted to fly over glaciers and icebergs or peer down into simmering volcanoes. I was therefore intrigued and wanted to know more. Luckily I didn't have to ask them to elaborate.

"Are you aware that a light aircraft disappeared over the Strait five days ago?" Gudren asked.

"Of course," I said. "According to the news that it was a six-seater Beech with three people on board. The pilot and two businessmen. I know the search operation lasted two days and there was no sign of the wreck."

"That's correct," Gudren said. "The pilot was putting out a distress call when communication was lost. It's believed there was engine failure and they either crashed or were forced down in a blizzard."

"So what has it got to do with you and your company?"

"It was our plane," Gudren said. "The two passengers on board were senior executives with the company. They'd been attending an energy conference in Reykjavik and were on their way to visit one of our gas production facilities above the Arctic Circle."

"And you think the body that's turned up could be one of your people?"

She nodded. "Viktor and I work for the company's global security division. We both know the executives and the pilot personally. They were our friends. We were told to come down here in the hope that we might be able to help solve the mystery. The families of the missing men are desperate to know what's happened. We've been liaising with the authorities but until Professor Brun contacted the police yesterday there had been no sightings."

"So how did the professor find the body?"

"He didn't. It was discovered by a group of Inuits who were seal hunting. They took it to the station. Unfortunately the weather closed in soon afterwards and no one has been able to approach the island since then. But it's now beginning to clear and we're anxious to get there as soon as we can."

It was a plausible story. But it was conveyed in a way that lacked feeling. It was as though she'd been reading from a pre-prepared script. And that struck me as odd since those missing men were supposed to be her friends as well as her colleagues.

"What are the police doing?" I asked.

"We've been told they're sending a team of officers and forensics technicians from Nuuk, but not until at least lunchtime. Conditions on the west coast have grounded flights apparently."

"There's a police helicopter based here," I said.

"It's been out of action for a week," Gudren said. "We've checked. They're waiting for replacement rotor blades."

"Right," I said. "I see the problem."

I turned to look at the Norseman. Jensen and three of his men were unloading boxes and crates. A couple of dogs were barking at them. On the other side of the harbour the painted hull of the Russian ship gleamed brightly in the sunshine.

I did a quick calculation in my head and decided that three times my normal hourly rate would amount to a nice little earner. With luck I could be back in Reykjavik by the middle of the afternoon.

"So is it a deal, Mr Preston?" Sidorov said. "Are you prepared to take us to the island?"

I thought about it for a few seconds, trying to identify the reason I had misgivings about the trip. But I couldn't get a handle on it and so I told myself that I'd be crazy to turn down a big fat fee.

I held out my hand again and Sidorov took it.

"It's a deal," I said.

It was a decision I'd come to regret.

TWO

We were ready to leave half an hour later. Jensen had unloaded his gear and I'd filled the Norseman's fuel tank.

Gudren and Sidorov came back down to the jetty after checking out of the hotel. They were carrying backpacks and wearing woollen hats.

When they were strapped into their seats I got us underway. The sea was still calm inside the fjord and it was a smooth take-off.

We were soon heading north above one of the most spectacular and desolate regions on the planet. The rugged coastline of east Greenland stretches for about sixteen hundred miles and yet is home to only a few thousand people. That's because unlike the west coast the ice imprisons it for all but a few months of the year.

To our left was a stunning panorama of icy mountains with sharp peaks and great glaciers that descended from the ice cap and plunged into the sea.

To our right the Denmark Strait, littered with icebergs of all shapes and sizes. Some of them as big and grand as cathedrals. It's estimated that more than ten thousand of them break away each year from the glaciers along the coast. They're like great ice sculptures, pure works of art with a limited lifespan.

If this had been a sightseeing tour I would have been regaling my passengers with a bunch of colourful facts about what was down below. Most tourists were surprised to learn that over eighty per cent of Greenland is covered with ice. And that the indigenous people are now known as Inuits because the term Eskimo is considered by many to be offensive.

That was what I liked about the Arctic region. It was full of surprises. Every day there was something new to see or experience. But I sensed that on this trip my passengers were not going to want a running commentary, no matter how interesting and jolly I made it. Their mission was far too serious and I'd learned to trust my instincts when it came to customers.

I was a pilot with one of the budget airlines when I first came here. The company launched a scheduled service between London and Reykjavik. It was during one of the stopovers that I met Anna, a receptionist in a hotel, and fell in love.

Nine months later the airline went bust and I was made redundant. So I sold my home and came north to get married. Anna already had a house in the city so I used my redundancy to buy the plane.

The business we started was barely into its second year when she died. But during her illness she urged me to stick with it.

"You'll need something to focus on," she said. "And it will have to be something you enjoy. Something you're passionate about."

So I'd stuck with it, for her sake as well as my own. I'd made every effort to find out as much as I could about the region and its people in the hope that it would help me make a success of the business. And I was pretty sure that it had.

My passengers were a curious pair, I thought. Taciturn and intense. I wondered what their exact roles were within the 'global security division.' In fact I hadn't realized that investment management companies had security divisions. But then maybe it was necessary if they had offices, plants and facilities in remote parts of the world, like the Arctic.

Terrorism, social unrest and cyber villainy posed a constant threat to every big company and corporation these days. Having a dedicated team to deal with the problem on a permanent basis probably made a lot of sense.

Viktor Sidorov and Gudren Bragason made an unlikely team, though. Neither struck me as a typical security officer. I would have pegged him as a nightclub bouncer and her as a nurse or teacher.

I wondered how they got on together. Was there any chemistry between them? Did they have a personal as well as a business relationship?

It was a pity I couldn't show more interest in them, engage them in conversation to pass the time and enrich the experience. And at the same time satisfy my curiosity.

But due to the nature of this trip I didn't think that would be appropriate.

*

When we reached the island we very nearly passed over it. I knew it was down there, just inside the mouth of a half-mile wide fjord, but I couldn't see it for the fog which lay like a carpet between the sheer grey walls on either side. Up ahead the silvery white tongue of a giant glacier slunk down into the mist like a frozen snake.

"The professor told us that the fog had almost cleared," Sidorov said, clearly disappointed.

I wasn't surprised that it hadn't. The fog had probably formed quickly, a not uncommon occurrence in Greenland where sea mist and land fog rise in summer almost as often as the sun itself.

From what I remembered Mikkelson Island was completely flat, except for a steep rocky hill that rose to about a hundred feet. The island itself was only a quarter of a mile in diameter.

"So what do we do now?" Gudren said.

I pointed out to sea. "We'll go out beyond the head of the fjord. It's clear out there and there isn't much ice around. I'll take her down and taxi up to the island. Don't worry. This isn't a problem."

It wouldn't be without risk once we got into the fog, though. But given the circumstances I felt it was a risk worth taking.

I took us out over the Strait and down onto the water, well clear of the pack-ice. It was a gentle landing and thankfully there were no unpleasant surprises. We then crawled slowly into the fjord.

The sun was still blazing high to our right. Its reflection revealed gently rising swells which I hadn't noticed before and I hoped it was an indication that the fog might be short-lived.

No one spoke as we entered the fog and I could almost feel the tension radiating from my passengers as the first fronds of vapour reached out towards us. Large floating chunks of ice appeared soon enough, but they were thin and brittle and easily thrust aside by the floats.

Visibility wasn't too bad considering and it was an immense relief when after a few minutes the shoreline appeared.

I ran the Norseman up onto a small beach, floats raising ridges in the shingle. When I shut off the engine a strange, unearthly silence enveloped us.

"So how far away is the station?" Sidorov asked.

"We follow the shore eastwards," I said. "It's a tiny island so it won't take us long to get there."

I lowered myself to the beach and opened the passenger door for the rest of them.

"Why don't you stay here, Mr Preston," Gudren said. "We won't be long."

"I'd rather not," I said. "I don't want to pass up the opportunity to meet the professor."

I could have sworn I detected a flash of disappointment in her eyes. But I chose to ignore it.

"Come on," I said. "Follow me."

We didn't have far to trek. After about five minutes I saw a light up ahead. The tiny yellow dot grew into a lamp above the door of the station's main cabin.

"Is this it?" Sidorov said, as if he'd expected much more.

"This is it," I said.

We made our way down a tricky slope where we came across other signs of civilisation. There was a stockpile of jerry cans, an upturned rowing boat and a couple of rusty old shovels. The cabin was a single-storey wooden affair on stone foundations, and needless to say, it was painted red.

The door opened suddenly as we approached, creaking on its hinges. Framed in the doorway was the strangest looking man I had ever seen. In fact to say that he was a man at that stage might have been jumping to conclusions. Anything could conceivably have been hiding behind that long white beard that trailed all the way down to his trouser belt.

"Hello, my friends," he boomed in a deep husky voice. "I heard your aircraft and wondered where you had got to."

The professor was a tall old bean but as thin as a matchstick. He was wearing a long-sleeved shirt under a tight waistcoat and grubby grey flannel trousers. His hair, or what little there was of it, was as frosted as his beard.

The room was just how I remembered it, with so many things around it was some time before my eyes could take in even half of it. Most of the junk was on the walls, shelves bending perceptibly under the weight of dozens of food tins and hardback books. In the few places where the wall itself showed through you could see that the green paint was peeled and blistered.

"Please forgive the mess," the professor said apologetically. "The rest of the team have been in the field for a couple of days so I'm all alone here and I'm not the tidiest of people."

Gudren introduced herself to the professor and then introduced Sidorov and me.

"I've heard a lot about you professor," I said. "It's good to meet you at last."

"You too, Mr Preston. I'm sorry I wasn't able to warn you about the fog. I thought it was clearing earlier."

"Not to worry," I said. "It's less dense than it looks from here."

Gudren then asked him if he had heard anything more from the police.

He nodded. "They told me a short time ago that they will be here at mid-day."

"Did you mention that we were coming to look at the body?"

"No, I didn't. Should I have?"

Gudren smiled. "Not at all. I was just curious."

The professor asked if any of us wanted coffee.

Gudren shook her head. "Thank you but no. We would rather see the body and be on our way. If the dead man is one of our colleagues then we shall need to make arrangements to inform his family and set wheels in motion."

The professor nodded. "Of course, I understand. We've left the poor man out back under a tarpaulin."

"Was he carrying any identification?" I asked.

"I'm afraid not," the professor said. "I searched his pockets and found nothing."

"What was he wearing?" Gudren asked.

"A leather jacket, sweater and trousers. But the clothes have been badly torn."

Gudred took a breath. "May we see him now? If we're able to identify him then it will save the police a lot of time and effort."

"Quite so," the professor said. "But be warned – he's not a pretty sight."

The professor turned and started walking towards a door at the rear. I held back to begin with, unsure what to do. But curiosity got the better of me and I followed them out back into an open storage area.

*

Wooden crates were piled high on one side of the yard and on the other there were two large fuel tanks and a generator. Beyond the yard was a small wooden out-building and a radio mast.

The body had been placed on a wooden table next to the generator. A heavy tarpaulin sheet had been draped over it.

"The police told me to leave him outside," the professor said. "The low temperatures will slow the decomposition process."

We gathered around the table and the professor pulled back the sheet. Gudren let out a gasp and I felt my stomach clench. I had to supress a sudden wave of nausea.

The body was face up. A man in his forties. Black hair. Athletic build. About six feet tall. His eyes were closed and his skin was the colour of sour milk. Part of his bottom lip was missing and there was a gash above his right eye. But what blood had been produced by the wounds had been washed away.

"The Inuits who brought him here found him among the floes," the professor said. "They say the injuries were almost certainly caused by the ice. They believe he drowned. I examined him briefly but saw no wounds that might have proved fatal. In other words I don't think he was a victim of foul play."

Sidorov stepped forward and leaned over the body. He said, "It looks to me as though he hasn't been dead for very long."

The professor nodded. "I agree. I'm not an expert in these matters but I would estimate that he was only in the water for a day or two."

"So you think it's unlikely he died as long ago as five days?" Sidorov said.

"The police asked me the same question so I take it you're all wondering if he was on the plane that was reported lost over the Strait almost a week ago."

"That's right," Sidorov said. "As we explained on the phone it belonged to our company."

The professor shrugged. "Well if this man was on that aircraft then he somehow managed to survive out on the water for perhaps three or four days. I can't imagine how. Conditions in the Strait have been awful this past week."

I ran my eyes along the length of the corpse. There were no rings on the guy's fingers, but he *was* wearing a wrist watch. The glass face was smashed and the brown leather strap was badly discoloured.

"So do you recognise him?" I asked, surprised that neither Sidorov nor Gudren had confirmed whether or not the dead man was one of their executives or the pilot of the company plane.

Sidorov gave an emphatic shake of his head. "No, he is not one of our people, thank God."

A thought struck me and I reached for the watch.

"What are you doing?" Gudren asked.

"Checking to see if there's an inscription on the back," I said.

Removing the watch was not a pleasant task but it proved to be worth it. There was indeed an inscription on the back. It read: *To Maxwell from Jean xx.*

"Bingo," I said.

The professor virtually grabbed the watch from me and examined it through squinting eyes.

"My God, you're right," he said. "Why didn't I think of that?"

I shrugged. "I have two watches and they were both birthday gifts. Each of them has an inscription so I thought it was worth checking."

The professor handed the watch to Gudren who in turn showed it to Sidorov.

"Well at least we have a name now," the professor said. "When you've gone I'll contact the police and let them know."

The professor pulled the tarpaulin back over the corpse and we paraded back into the cabin.

There was an air of unreality about what was happening. The experience was beginning to unsettle me and I was looking forward to getting home.

Gudren thanked the professor for letting us see the body and declined another offer of coffee.

"We need to get back to Reykjavik," she said.

The professor wished us a pleasant journey and we left him standing on the porch. When we reached the Norseman Gudren said she had left her gloves in the cabin. I was surprised because I hadn't noticed her wearing any. Sidorov offered to go back to the cabin to get them for her. While he was gone we climbed on board and I got to work warming up the engine.

When Sidorov came back ten minutes later we got under way. Beyond the mouth of the fjord I took her up and steered an easterly course out across the Strait.

We passed over the broken pack ice and the wider iceberg lanes that revealed clearly the steady movement of the Greenland Current.

I tried to make conversation with my two passengers, thinking that they'd be more relaxed now that they knew the dead man on Mikkelson island was not one of their company executives or the pilot. But they were still tense and uncommunicative, so I thought maybe they had both been profoundly affected by the sight of the corpse.

We approached Iceland two hours later. The rugged, mountainous island lifted out of the sea quite suddenly. When we were near enough I eased the stick forward and lost some altitude as the majestic black cliffs of the coast rolled by beneath us. We were over that land of extraordinary contradictions, where stunning glaciers are neighbours to hot springs and black deserts, where active volcanoes pock mark the landscape and rear up alongside green, fertile valleys.

I took us in over the tip of the Snoefellsness peninsula, beyond which lie the shimmering waters of Faxa Bay, then set her on a course for the domestic airport.

That's when Sidorov said, "You can turn here, Preston. Head east along the coast."

"But that's the wrong way," I said.

"Just do as you're told."

The sharp tone of his voice prompted me to turn and as I did so my blood froze.

He was holding a revolver and it was pointing at my face.

THREE

I knew straight away that the Russian was deadly serious. His face was set in grim determination and his eyes were cold and callous.

I took my headset off and said, "What the fuck is this?"

His voice was hard, cruel. "Don't argue. Just change course."

"But I don't understand."

"You aren't meant to," he said. "And leave the headset off. If you try to use the radio I'll rip it out."

The hand that held the gun was very steady and the little hole at the end of the barrel was only inches from my forehead. I don't know much about guns, but I'd seen and heard about the one he carried. It was a Colt 45 automatic and by all accounts it's a real man stopper, which from point-blank range can tear a hole in you big enough for a rabbit to crawl through.

I faced forward and desperately tried to steady my hands on the controls — an impossible endeavour if there ever was one. I changed course and took her in towards the coast at full throttle.

"There's a headland up ahead," Sidorov said. "Take us down on this side of it."

The headland was slightly to our left. I started to turn in my seat, intent on conveying some sort of protest, but I felt the gun against the nape of my neck and had second thoughts about it.

I managed to take us down without losing control of the Norseman, which in the circumstances was no mean achievement. The touch down, however, wouldn't have won me any prizes, but then I challenge anyone to retain his equanimity with a gun on him.

Water splashed over the windscreen as the float cut through the swell. I brought the bird to a stop about a hundred yards offshore. The water was ice free and relatively calm.

The desolate coastline was inhabited only by screaming gulls and swarms of proud little puffins. There were no cliffs, except to our right where the headland jutted out into the bay like the fossilised foot of an ancient giant. On this side of the headland the view was taken up by a steep grass-covered hill that dropped onto a long stony beach.

"What now?" I said.

"We wait," Sidorov replied.

"But what's this about?"

"Just be quiet. If you say nothing and do nothing then you will probably live through this. If not you'll die."

Sidorov still had the gun on me and I knew from that range a baby couldn't miss. My heart thudded relentlessly inside my chest. I was scared. More scared than I had ever been in my entire life.

We sat in silence for the best part of a minute and I tried to figure things out, but it was no good; nothing made sense except the hopelessness of the situation.

I turned to look at Gudren, or whatever her bloody name was. She was peering out the window, her jaw set tight.

"Would you please explain to me what's going on?" I pleaded. "Who the hell are you people?"

She moved her head to look at me. There was a hard edge to her features that I hadn't seen before.

"You've been warned, Preston," she said. "Say another word and you'll regret it."

My spine grew rigid and a cold sweat formed on my brow. My plane had effectively been hijacked and I was now being threatened. But why for pity's sake? What did these two weirdoes hope to achieve? And why were we just sitting here? Was something about to happen?

Outside the sweltering heat of the cabin, the sea stretched away westwards with no sign of life on it. That high promontory of land cut off a lot of the view, including all the boats I'd seen from above. The land showed no sign of life either, apart from the birds. There was only the beach and a scattering of rocks along it.

Then I saw a movement up ahead. A small boat was rounding the tip of the headland. Sidorov saw it too and said, "It's them."

As far as I could make out it was a fishing boat with a dark green hull and as it neared I glimpsed a figure on the forward deck outlined against the sky. He certainly wasn't an Icelandic fisherman unless they'd suddenly taken to wearing tapered suits in place of sou'westers and bulky jerseys.

The boat was about thirty yards away when I managed to pick out the name painted on the bow in bold blue. It was *Hekla* — after Iceland's famous volcano of the same name.

I didn't see it draw any closer for just then I felt a searing pain at the back of my head. It was as if an explosion had shattered the skull into a thousand pieces. An image of something red flashed before my eyes and then, quite suddenly, there was nothing. Nothing, that is, but the darkness.

*

Something was burning. I could tell that much even though I couldn't be sure who I was. The acrid smell of smoke and fumes was unmistakeable. I could even taste it, deep in my throat and as bitter as acid. I was crawling out of a cave, a deep, dark cave full of black figures and voices where even the bats were afraid. I clawed at the ground, pulling myself with agonizing slowness towards a little gleam of light that burned far ahead. The light turned out to be a hole at the end of a dream and I crawled through it.

Slowly, painfully my eyes creaked open and I found myself staring up at an undulating mass of metallic grey. The colour and the distance told me it was the familiar low-slung ceiling of the Norseman.

I raised my head with some difficulty and tried to absorb with one quick glance what was happening to me, but it was like looking through a steamed-up window. I closed my eyes for a spell and tried again. Everything was still blurred, but I could see enough to know I was slumped across the front seats of the seaplane. I hauled myself up and craned my neck to look behind me.

That's when I saw a small orange flame   crawling down the inside of the fuselage along a strangled white sheet that was hanging from a broken window. The end was knotted and resting on the floor.

At once I realized its significance and I tensed. My first instinct was to reach for my mobile phone to raise the alarm. But it wasn't where it should have been in my pocket.

Then I noticed the pools of dark liquid on the seats and floor. I didn't need to be told it was petrol. The pungent smell hit me like a hard slap.

But my strength had been sapped by the crushing blow Sidorov had delivered and I found it difficult to extricate myself from the seat harness.

Once I'd managed it I tried to shift open the door, but it wouldn't budge. Just then a great sheet of flame reared up from behind the seats. I knew I didn't have much time. The fire was taking hold in a big way and moving towards me.

With an almighty effort I jerked down the handle and threw my shoulder at the door. This time it gave under the pressure and I went crashing through. I landed with a painful wallop on the port float and rolled into the icy sea.

The cold water brought me rapidly to my senses and prevented me from panicking in an effort to get quickly to the surface. Instead, I held my breath and propelled myself downwards, deeper, clawing at the void that was the sea.

It didn't take long for the plane to go up. The water muffled the sound of the explosion, but even so it was loud enough to make me realize that it must have been a hell of a blast.

I braced myself, though kept going, kicking with tired legs and hoping to God there was enough oxygen in me to stave off the onset of asphyxia.

When the force of the explosion hit me it was like a tidal wave, lifting me over and over with terrifying ease. My body had no will of its own, no feeling, as it spun, twisted and somersaulted through the water.

I thought I was going to drown, but then, thank God, I felt myself slowing. Soon I was floating through water made opaque by the penetrating rays of the sun.

But as my senses returned, one by one, I realized it still wasn't over — not by a long way. I could feel my insides bursting, the pressure building up to an explosive degree.

Desperate for air, I began to race upwards. I hadn't gone down very far, perhaps twelve feet, but it seemed more like twelve miles. Every second dragged by and all the time I was on the verge of opening my mouth to liberate the monster that was growing inside me.

But I made it, and as I broke surface, choking and spluttering, I drew in an enormous chunk of air that made me dizzy. I managed to keep calm, though, and let myself float, eyes shut tight, until it passed. I swallowed air until it bloated me and then set about achieving a normal rate of breathing.

I looked around, my head just above water. The blazing Norseman was only yards away. A pall of thick black smoke rose above her. Flames stabbed at the sky, spitting shoals of sparks into the air. For several hundred yards in every direction there were parts of the wreckage, black shapes bobbing with the swells. But there was no sign of the boat.

I turned full circle, but still I couldn't see her. I didn't think they could have gone far, for I doubted that I'd been unconscious longer than a few minutes and I assumed they had used the sheet as a fuse to allow them to get a safe distance from the blast.

I realized then that I'd suffered a terrible loss. The Norseman was my only source of income. She was insured, of course, but that wasn't the point. It would be a long time before she could be replaced.

I stopped thinking about it when I saw the fishing boat on the other side of the inferno. It was shifting away from me, a slipstream of bubbling white foam trailing behind. I stayed where I was, treading water and half hidden by the smoke from the wreckage.

There was about a hundred yards of water between myself and dry land and I hoped I had the strength to make it before flaking out.

The fishing boat hadn't quite rounded the headland when I decided to make a move. I couldn't wait any longer because the energy I was using up was far too precious. And the cold was eating into my muscles.

I started swimming, alternating between breast stroke and crawl. I didn't look back after that, just swam as hard and as fast as I could, which was about as fast as a channel swimmer covering those last hundred yards to a French beach. The water was freezing and my body felt as if it had been trampled on by a herd of buffalo.

At last, having almost reached the point of collapse, my feet touched the bottom and I staggered onto the beach, collapsing face down on the stones. I lay there like a stranded piece of driftwood, my face buried in sharp, cutting shingle.

It was some moments before I found the energy to turn over. I opened my eyes and stared up at a cloudless sky. A wind was up, blowing from the west in sharp, cold blasts that made me shiver under the wet clothes. Then I pushed myself to a sitting position and looked out to sea.

"Oh shit!"

The boat had turned around and was now bearing down on the beach, foam curling around the bow as she drew inexorably nearer. She couldn't have been more than a hundred yards offshore so I assumed she had changed course soon after I'd started swimming for it.

I heaved myself up and began to evaluate my chances. They weren't good. The hill rose steadily behind me, but it offered not a vestige of cover. Along the beach there were some rocks climbing almost to the crest of the hill. After a quick glance at the approaching boat I scrambled towards them, feet sinking into the shingle.

On reaching the rocks I threw myself to the ground between two big basalt boulders and lay there face down for several seconds listening to the wild thumping of my own heart. Then I sat up, pushed my back against one of the boulders and looked up.

The rocks were not as closely clustered as they had seemed from afar and there were large areas of open grass between them. So for the most part I'd be presenting a target as big as the proverbial barn door. I prayed that Sidorov was not in possession of a high-powered rifle.

I took a few deep breaths to fill my lungs, then sprang to my feet and started off. I struggled from rock to rock in a zig-zag pattern, stopping only briefly to catch my breath.

By the time I reached the top of the hill the boat had stopped just offshore and two men were making for the beach in an outboard powered dinghy. I recognized one of them as Sidorov. The other man, looking dapper in a grey suit with open neck white shirt, I'd never seen before.

I wasted no time watching them. Turning, I discovered that the hill dropped slightly on the other side before the land became flat and treeless right up to the distant mountains. Away to my right were the bright red roofs of some farm buildings.

As is typical of Icelandic farms there was a labyrinth of carefully constructed drainage ditches spreading out from it. One of the ditches cut through the land not far from where I was standing, snaking both towards the farm and away from it across a field.

I began running. The ground was hard and uneven, having been buckled into tussocks by the winter frost. I stumbled several times and once landed on a sharp stone that cut through my jacket and grazed my right elbow.

On reaching the ditch I plunged straight in. It was deeper than I expected. About eight feet down I landed with a splash in about six inches of muddy water. But luckily I didn't hurt myself and somehow managed to stay on my feet.

But just ahead the ditch curved sharply and I was suddenly confronted with a wall of earth.

I carried on running and jumped up at it, clawing frantically with stiffened fingers. I found a small jutting rock and managed to get a purchase on it with my left foot. I put all my weight onto it and heaved. Both hands found something to grab and I started to pull myself up.

My arms were just over the top of the ditch when a shot rang out behind me.

FOUR

He was well within range when he fired and the bullet bulldozed into the earth only inches from my right ear.

I pulled myself over the edge and, lying flat, risked a quick look back over my shoulder. The pair of them were running towards me and the gap between us was no more than about fifty yards. There was about the same distance between myself and the farm, and that too was over flat, open ground.

I struggled to my feet and ran, veering from side to side like a drunken athlete. I suppose I wasn't an easy target, because they didn't try to pick me off, or if they did I didn't hear the shot above my own panting.

I wasn't running fast. I couldn't. Maybe someone who had trained for months could have kept going like the clappers to the very end, but not someone who couldn't even remember the last time he'd exercised his limbs. It seemed as if my legs were hanging off and I was merely dragging them along behind me.

I could see five low-slung buildings. They were made of wood, painted white and fashioned to typical Icelandic standards with pointed roofs and small square windows. There was one large building with a smaller one facing it across a yard and the others stood to one side of them forming a U shape.

I swung round the first of the buildings, putting it between me and my pursuers. In the building on the other side of the yard there was a door half open. There were curtains in the windows so I assumed it was the farmer's house. The building I was next to turned out to be the barn. The large double doors were gaping wide just ahead, revealing a gloomy interior. It would have been the obvious place to hide and I was sure Sidorov would have thought so too. So I made for the house.

I got there and managed to close the door behind me just as they came around the side of the barn. I stood peering through the curtains, sure that everyone for a mile around could hear my heavy breathing.

Sidorov and his friend halted and tried to decide which way I'd gone. Sidorov's face was set in a mean, twisted expression; lips pulled tight across his teeth. The other bloke was about thirty-five with closely set eyes and a nose that was flattened to his face. They moved forward circumspectly, two men with death in their eyes. Then Sidorov said something to the other man who nodded a reply. They split up, Sidorov going towards the barn, his pal edging over towards me.

I turned and found I was in a short carpeted passage with five closed doors. The first two I tried gave access to the kitchen and bathroom. The third let me into the living room and I closed it behind me. It was a quaint little room full of old-world charm, and French windows let in plenty of light. There was a big stone fireplace and a low coffee table in the middle of the floor. On the table a bowl of fruit and a large ornate onyx table lighter. A set of keys next to the lighter caught my eye. I scooped them up. Two keys on a ring fashioned into a steering wheel.

I went over to the French windows. Beyond them was a small yard fronting the house with a narrow dirt track leading away from it. A mud-splattered Land Rover was parked in the yard. I started to slide back the glass door just as Sidorov's pal stepped into the room.

He saw me and his face grew a wide, sardonic grin. I looked at the gun in his hand and shivered. He came further into the room, stretched out his arm and took aim.

I could almost feel that cold ring of metal against my forehead. He closed one eye and screwed up the other.

I didn't know at the time what caused him to turn around at that precise moment and I didn't pause to find out. But in that split second as his head revolved towards the door I sprang halfway across the room. By the time he realized what was happening I was already lashing at his wrist with a clenched fist. He jerked his arm away from me and loosened his grip on the gun which went spinning from his hand.

I grabbed his wrist. His free arm wrapped itself around my neck and he began squeezing the life out of me. I was in no condition to wrestle standing up so with one mighty effort I pulled him into me and at the same time allowed myself to topple backwards.

We went crashing down on top of the coffee table which collapsed under us, then rolled over towards the fireplace like a pair of hard at it lovers. His teeth gnawed into my neck and his knee swiped at my groin. He was easily getting the better of me.

Then I saw the lighter, its big onyx stand glinting like an emerald eye. I reached for it, closed my fingers around it, then forced my chest up and lifted the lighter above his head. I brought it down a second later. It caught him just above the left eye. Blood spurted everywhere from a deep gash and he let go of my neck before letting out an agonising scream. But the bastard kept going, his face an ugly mask of pain.

The next blow had all my reserve strength behind it and it did the job. It left a big red dent in the middle of his forehead. His body convulsed violently, a horrible gasp forced his lips apart and he went limp. I dropped the lighter and struggled to my feet. His chest was still rising and falling so he wasn't dead, which was a bloody pity. I turned around as the sweat from my forehead began to sting my eyes.

There was a little girl standing in the doorway. Her eyes were wide and staring and her skin was a sickly white. She was no more than eight and I wondered how many nightmares this little scene would cause her to have.

She was wearing a pretty pink nightdress and we had probably woken her from an afternoon nap. I owed my life to the fact that she had entered the room at that particular moment. I smiled at her, but she found no reassurance in that. Her eyes remained transfixed on the figure at my feet. I was tempted to take her in my arms then, but there wasn't time and I'm sure she wouldn't have understood anyway. So I turned and got the hell out of there.

I ran to the nearest door of the Land Rover, praying the keys I had would start it. It was open and I jumped in. The first key I tried in the ignition didn't fit but the other slid in beautifully. As the engine fired I released the handbrake and shoved her into gear. Just as the Land Rover lurched forward the windscreen was shattered. I didn't hear the shot and I didn't look to see how far away he was. I stamped on the accelerator and punched a hole in the broken glass.

I got quickly into second and swung the wheel around so that Sidorov would have to shoot at the back of the vehicle. I was soon into third and then into fourth, glancing in the mirror frequently at the receding view of the farm. Sidorov, almost lost in a cloud of dust, was standing with his arms dangling at his sides, gun pointing to the ground.

It was a bumpy ride to the end of the track and by the time I got there my backside was raw. The farm was about five hundred yards behind me and there was a wide asphalt road going both ways. I turned right and settled back, wondering how far I was from the nearest town. I didn't try to think beyond that as I drove.

Soon my heart beat dropped to around one-fifty and my muscles freed themselves from the iron grip of tension. Gradually, though, the scars of battle began to make themselves known, aches and pains in every fibre of my being and when I felt the back of my head I discovered an enormous lump dissected by a shallow gash from which blood trickled.

44

I was conscious of the road winding around the edge of a fjord, then dipping into a valley rich in crops and grass. I passed several farms and a sign which told me I was only five kilometres from Reykjavik. Once there I intended going straight to the police. There was still time to intercept the boat.

But as I approached a blind junction I was going at close on fifty. Too bloody fast. I pressed down hard on the brakes just as a small white van came tearing out from behind the high earth mound bordering the road.

My only thought was to avoid a collision. I twisted the wheel and the earth mound charged at me.

FIVE

At first the voice was faint and distant. Above the ringing in my ears it made no sense. It was just a muffled sound out there in the dark. I felt myself reaching out towards it, at the same time trying to free my body from the black shroud that had wrapped itself around me. Eventually I realized it was the voice of a woman, a stranger, and she was calling to me.

"Mr Preston. Are you awake? Can you hear me?"

I felt pressure on my left arm. Her hands were warm, fingers soft and smooth.

"Mr Preston, can you hear me?"

I surfaced from the blackness quite suddenly, cold and wet. I had to force my eyelids open; it felt as if they had been stuck down with hard setting glue.

At first everything was a meaningless blur, the girl a dark image against the rippling white of the ceiling. Gradually she was drawn into focus and I discovered she was leaning over me with a big bright smile on her face, her hair pushed out of sight under a funny looking white hat.

"How do you feel?" she said gently.

"Terrible," I croaked.

And it was no exaggeration. If I looked anything like I felt then I wasn't a pretty sight. My head was splitting and there was a dull, aching sensation in my chest.

Her smile became a chuckle. "I'm not surprised. You have quite a nasty bump on your head."

I thought of the obvious question and asked it. "Where am I?"

"The City Hospital, Reykjavik. You were involved in an automobile accident."

I blinked, confused. There was a bitter taste in my mouth and my lips were dry and cracked.

"We found your wallet in your pocket," she said. "That's how we were able to identify you."

I said weakly, "Could I have a drink of water?"

"Of course. Can you sit up?"

I sat up and she supported me with one hand while she plumped up the pillows with the other. I felt sick and shaky. There was a jug of water on the bedside table. The nurse filled a glass and handed it to me. I drank half of it before coming up for air, then looked around. It was a small, clinical room and I had it to myself. There were no blood-drips or any other life-saving contraptions attached to me, so I assumed I wasn't in such a bad way. I emptied the glass in another swig and passed it back to the nurse.

"Better?"

"Much," I said. "Thanks."

She placed the glass back on the table and eyed me curiously. She had a pretty face, young and soft with a freckly nose. Her skin was pale and flawless. But I could tell that her smile was getting strained.

I let out my breath slowly, said, "How did I get here?"

"Ambulance. You were lucky there was another motorist nearby at the time."

A bout of trembling gripped me.

"Am I okay?" I asked.

She nodded. "There's nothing seriously wrong with you I'm happy to say. Some cuts and bruises, but nothing that won't heal itself."

"My chest hurts."

"You have a large bruise there."

It came back to me then in a sudden flood of recollection that left me stunned and sweating. I wondered briefly if it had all been a dream. Perhaps, I thought vaguely, the whole terrible episode which had begun in Tasiilaq had been entirely conjured up by the sub-conscious. But then a quick appraisal of the situation I was now in, and the pain I felt, convinced me otherwise.

"The police," I whispered urgently. "I must speak to them."

Her face did not even register surprise. Checking that the sheets were tucked in on her side of the bed, she said, "Do you feel up to it right now?"

"Sure. Can you get me a phone?"

"There's no need. A policeman is outside now. He's been waiting for you to wake."

"How long has he been here?"

"Several hours. He arrived shortly after you were brought in."

"What time is it?"

She consulted her pocket watch. "Seven in the evening."

"Oh Christ." About five hours had passed since the accident and by now Sidorov and his psycho companions would be long gone.

"Can I see him now?" I said.

"I'll have to check with the doctor first."

She'd been gone about a minute when a man in a white coat entered with a uniformed police officer. White coat was middle-aged and wore a pair of horn-rimmed glasses that gave him an air of placid respectability. The policeman was a different proposition. Thick-set and rough-looking, there was nothing in either his face or his manner that indicated a friendly nature.

White coat smiled. "How are you feeling, Mr Preston?"

"My head aches and I'm confused," I said. "But from what the nurse told me I'm lucky to be alive."

"That's true enough. No serious damage was done to you in the accident."

"That's a relief."

"I'm doctor Gelling. This is Constable Jonsson. He would like a word with you." The doctor came forward and checked my pulse. "We'd like you to stay with us overnight just so that we can keep an eye on you for a while."

"I thought you said there was nothing seriously wrong."

"And so there isn't. But we do like to make sure that our patients are completely well before they go home. And we'll be monitoring you for any delayed reaction."

He gave my wrist back and went on, "I've stitched a cut at the back of your head. The lump on your forehead will heal by itself. And the same goes for the bruising on your chest. Would you like to tell us what happened?"

"Someone tried to kill me," I said.

The cop's hard, sullen face remained impassive but the doctor arched his brow.

I looked at the cop and said, "Is that why you're here? Have they been caught?" I knew it was wishful thinking on my part.

"Have who been caught?" the cop said.

"The men who tried to kill me," I responded sharply.

He shot a glance at the doctor and I didn't need him to spell it out.

"No, I'm not off my rocker," I snapped. "Somebody did try to kill me. How do you think I ended up here?"

"You stole a Land Rover and then crashed it," the cop said.

So that was why he was here. I felt my throat tighten.

"I had to take it," I told him. "They were chasing me with guns."

"Why?"

"I don't frigging know."

"Who were they?"

"I don't know that either."

"So two men you don't know tried to kill you for no reason."

I could tell by the tone of his voice that he was thinking the knock to the head had done more than just cause a swelling. He stepped closer to the bed, removed his hat. He had thick, fair hair and a high forehead.

"Now what about the Land Rover?" he asked.

"The Land Rover isn't important you bloody idiot," I said. "Someone tried to kill me I'm telling you. Can't you get that into your thick skull?"

He took a deep breath and pulled a notebook from his pocket. Then he narrowed his gaze and said, "So tell me what happened to you."

So I told him. It didn't take long. I condensed the whole incredible sequence of events into as few words as possible. As I spoke I could feel my gut tighten another notch.

When I was through the cop finished scribbling in his notebook and said, "Are these people Icelandic?"

"The woman is, or at least I think she is. But Sidorov is Russian. I'm sure of it."

"And the man in the suit?"

"I don't know. I didn't hear him speak."

"This boat - did it have a name?"

"Yes. It was *Hekla* — after the volcano."

"Can anyone corroborate your story?"

I felt a sinking despair. The idiot still wasn't convinced.

"There's the little girl at the farm," I said. "She saw the fight. Didn't the farmer tell you?"

51

"He did say there was a fight of some kind in his house, but he was in the basement and by the time he emerged it was over and you'd gone. There was no one else there. He said his daughter was hysterical and he couldn't get any sense out of her."

"Surely you can see now why I took the Land Rover," I said. "I had no choice. The bastards were trying to shoot me."

"If your story is true then yes it does make sense."

"Of course it's true," I said. "Why would I make it up?"

The doctor stepped forward and took my wrist in a strong but gentle grip. "Please, Mr Preston, try not to excite yourself."

"Then tell this moron to do what he's paid to do. While he's standing there shaking his head at me those characters are roaming the streets."

The cop stared at me for a long moment, then sighed. "Very well, Mr Preston. I'll look into your story, but let me tell you this. If you've lied to conceal the fact that you stole .."

I raised my hand to shut him up. "No need to tell me anything," I said. "Just take my word for it and find those bastards."

*

Later during the evening I was moved to a ward and given pyjamas and a gaudy black and white striped dressing gown that was about three sizes too big. Then they gave me some food, which wasn't at all bad, before another nurse tucked me in for the night and wished me pleasant dreams. It was all rather cosy, but I didn't feel much like sleeping and I was sure that my dreams would not be pleasant.

I tried for a while, rolling into every conceivable position from crouching on my side to smothering my face in the pillows. I didn't think it would work and I was right. The usual collection of night noises didn't help. Two beds away some old timer had an itch in his throat and no amount of coughing and spluttering could rid him of it.

Further along the row on my side of the ward a younger man obviously had bladder trouble and every time he got the urge he made a point of announcing the fact with a few well chosen curses in Icelandic as he hurried along the ward.

Finally I got fed up with lying there, climbed out of bed and slipped on the dressing gown.

I shuffled into the corridor. It was chillier there and the floor tiles were like ice against my feet. I was in just the mood for a stiff drink, but I doubted that the hospital would oblige, so I decided to pass sometime in the recreation room at the end of the corridor. I opened the door, switched on the light and went in.

There wasn't much in there; a couple of winged armchairs around a low glass coffee table and a television perched on a high wooden stand. But the window covered almost the entire wall and offered a panoramic view of the city. I closed the door and settled in one of the chairs.

Within a short time I was feeling less tense and considerably more relaxed.

For a while I tried to figure out a logical explanation for what had happened, but I couldn't. The obvious question was why had they tried to kill me? It could not have been for any personal reason because they didn't know me. No, it had to be something else and I was betting that it was connected to the corpse I'd taken them to see. But why had they decided to kill me? Were they afraid I would say something to the authorities about what happened on the island? If so then what the hell was it? After all, nothing much happened except that they looked at a dead man and decided he was not one of their colleagues. But then how much of the story they told me had been true?

Eventually I succeeded in putting these thoughts to one side. I put my feet up on the radiator under the window and slumped back in the chair. It was still light outside thanks to the midnight sun. This was something I had never really got used to.

Anna and I had always tried to make the most of the endless daylight. Romantic evening flights, lakeside picnics, basking in the hot springs. Life was really good back then and the future was bright and full of hope.

We talked about buying a bigger house and starting a family. Two children, we decided. Maybe even a dog.

But then the symptoms started to kick in. The tiredness. The coughing. The sore throats. The chest pains.

The doctors diagnosed her with lung cancer and within three months she was dead. It was heart breaking to watch her deteriorate and to know that she had brought it on herself by smoking heavily since she was a teenager. But at least the end came relatively quickly. She didn't have to suffer for many months or years on end.

It took me a long time to function properly after she was gone. The sadness lingered for months and the grief was all-consuming. Her presence was everywhere. I could feel her close to me in the house. Even in our bed. And I could smell the smoke from her cigarettes.

At one point I decided to return to England. But I couldn't bring myself to leave the country where my dear wife was buried. So I changed my mind and stayed on.

And despite what had happened since this morning I was glad that I did – because no matter how bad things got for me I would always find comfort in the knowledge that Anna was close by.

*

A flashing blue light woke me. It struck against the outside of the window every other second, splashing colour into the room. I rubbed both eyes briskly with my knuckles and a quick glance at the wall clock told me I'd been asleep for about an hour. Still feeling drowsy, I pushed myself up and looked out of the window. On the forecourt below there was a parked police car with its siren light flashing.

After a stretch and a yawn I left the room and padded towards the ward. I heard voices as I approached. Words were being exchanged with no consideration for the sleeping patients. As I passed the ward office I looked in. Doctor Gelling was in there arguing with Constable Jonsson and the night nurse was standing between them red-faced and stiff as a tree.

When she saw me her mouth fell open, her eyes all but popped out of their sockets and her expression ended abruptly the bickering between the two men. They followed her gaze to me.

"It's him," blurted the constable. He rushed forward and grabbed my right arm.

"Where have you been, Preston?" he demanded in faltering English.

"I fell asleep in the recreation room," I explained resentfully. "Why? What's all the excitement?"

The doctor came to my rescue. "Constable, please. Keep calm." To me, he said. "We thought you had run away."

"Why should I want to do that?"

"Don't pretend you don't know, Preston," the cop seethed.

I was about to counter with something suitably nasty when two other uniforms appeared out of nowhere and surrounded me.

"Call off the search," Jonsson told them. "We've got him. Tell the station I'm bringing him in."

SIX

The cell was small, no more than twelve feet by six, with bricked walls that had been painted chocolate brown by someone who clearly didn't take their work seriously. There was one small barred window installed so high up that to see through it you'd have needed a pair of firm stilts and a keen sense of balance.

Light trickled in almost reluctantly through a small glass panel above the door. It emanated from a single low-powered bulb in the corridor.

I was sitting on the only piece of furniture available, a hard wooden bench fixed to a concrete underside so it couldn't be moved. I'd already been in the cell an hour and nothing had happened except that a tiny winged insect had succeeded in meeting a rather sticky end by persistently landing on my nose. Now that he was gone I was alone again with nothing to do but stare at the opposite wall.

They'd told me nothing during the short drive to the Central Police Station. On arrival I was hauled out of the car and frog-marched into the building.

The clothes I was wearing added to my discomfort. My own stuff had been ruined so the hospital had come up with a thick polo sweater that was far too big and probably belonged to the giant who owned the striped dressing gown. The corduroy trousers were definitely not his, though; I suspected they had been donated to the hospital by some poor wretch who'd starved himself to death.

My thoughts strayed. I kept asking myself why I was so unpopular all of a sudden. I didn't have exceptionally bad breath that I was aware of and I couldn't recall ever spitting on the Bible. And yet the whole bloody world seemed to be ill-intentioned towards me — which was putting it mildly.

It was 2 a.m. when finally the cell door opened and two uniformed bulls told me to follow them. We set off in echelon along a cold concrete corridor, up two flights of stairs and at the end of another corridor we stopped outside someone's office. One of the uniforms knocked, then poked his head inside and beckoned me in.

It was a smartly furnished office with a carpet on the floor and a large steel-grey desk, behind which sat a couple of serious gents in plain clothes. There was a vacant chair on the other side of the desk facing them and without being asked I went and sat in it. My uniformed escort left the room, closing the door behind them.

For a long moment no one spoke, the pair of them sat motionless, studying me closely and I wondered if they were waiting for me to grow another head.

At last the one on the left said, "Care for a cigarette?"

"Just get to the point," I said. "Why am I here?"

A cool, confident grin spread its tentacles across his face. "My name is Kjarvel," he said. "I'm chief of police here in Reykjavik."

I didn't need to be told he was a high-ranking policeman. Like most of those who wield a certain amount of authority it showed quite clearly in his manner, just as rough, cracked hands expose a farmer or labourer for what he is.

He turned to the other man. "This is Inspector Geisler. He is with the Greenlandic police."

Geisler was fiftyish with a round shiny face and strong Inuit features.

I licked my dry lips, said, "Look, are you going to tell me what's going on?"

"You should know," Kjarvel said.

"All know is that I intend to sue you lot for false arrest."

"You aren't under arrest yet, Mr Preston," Kjarvel made clear.

"Well if that's so why did those goons drag me out of hospital?"

He lit himself a cigarette and spoke through the smoke. "You were required here in a hurry. But your doctor informed us that you were not seriously injured and therefore able to leave the hospital."

"So what's going on?" I said.

Kjarvel pursed his lips. "This story you told the constable. We want to hear it."

"Then I take it you don't believe me."

"I'll reserve my judgement until I've heard it from you," he said. "Now if you don't mind. It is rather late."

There was no point arguing; this game was played by their rules. So I ran through the tale again and Geisler pulled me up when I got to the part about the watch.

He said, "And you are sure the inscription on the back said to Maxwell from Jean?"

"I'm positive," I said.

I went on with the story right up to the present time. Afterwards Geisler got to his feet. He walked over to the window with a pronounced limp. His left leg appeared to be a couple of inches shorter than the right. Without turning from the window, he said, "Where are they now - Sidorov and the woman?"

"How should I know?" I said.

"They're your friends aren't they?"

He spun round to face me and something close to malice gleamed in his bloodshot eyes.

"I'd never met them before yesterday," I said. "I told you that. You should check with the people in Tasiilaq, including the hotel. Sidorov and Gudren were staying there and making it known they were desperate to get to the island. When I flew in yesterday the couple approached me. My friend Else Jensen can confirm it. So can Bill Osborn. He's a pilot like me. He was supposed to take them but he got drunk. There was no other means of transport until I turned up. "

"We're in contact with the officer who is based in the town," Geisler said. "We'll pass on those names to him right away. But I have to tell you that we've already checked parts of your story and they don't hold true."

Something heavy dropped to the bottom of my stomach and I wouldn't have been surprised if it was my heart.

"What do you mean?"

"For one thing there is no company called Polar Investments. And we have no record of anyone named Peter Sidorov or Gudren Bragason living or working here in Iceland."

"And that's not all," Kjarvel put in. "We traced the owner of that fishing boat you say you saw. The Hekla. He's assured us that it did not leave its mooring yesterday afternoon. We searched the boat, of course, but found nothing to corroborate your story."

"Then how come I knew there was such a boat?" I said.

"You probably picked on that name by chance," Kjarvel said. "In fact the only part of your story that does ring true is that your seaplane was burned out and you took the Land Rover after fighting with someone at the farm. But who's to say that you didn't set light to the plane yourself in order to collect the insurance?"

"Now hold on one minute," I said. "What exactly are you getting at here? Are you accusing me of something – apart from stealing a fucking Land Rover?"

Geisler stepped in front of me and stared down contemptuously.

"We're accusing you of murder, Preston. Cold blooded murder." He spat the words at me and I could almost feel their venomous sting. "The police found Professor Brun yesterday afternoon on the island. He'd been shot in the head. Whoever did it then burned down the station and destroyed the body that was recovered from the sea."

SEVEN

I sat there completely bewildered for all of a minute, but it took much longer for the full realization of what he'd said to sink in.

I could feel their eyes on me the whole time, trying to read into my expression something that wasn't there.

It still didn't make any sense to me. It just didn't seem possible that the professor was dead, murdered. I'd been with him and he had been very much alive such a short time ago.

"Why did you do it?" Geisler said.

I looked up into a pair of accusing eyes that were doing their best to melt my nerves. I could feel the alarm moving through my chest.

"I didn't do it." It was about all I could think of saying.

"Can you prove it?"

I couldn't and he knew it. I said, "What possible motive would I have for wanting him dead?"

"But he is dead," Geisler said. "He was murdered and by your own admission you were there when it happened."

"That's ridiculous. He was alive when we left there."

"You say you left at what time?" Geisler asked.

"It must have been ten-thirty or close to it," I said.

"Then it shouldn't surprise you to learn that it was about that time he was shot. The fire was still smouldering when the police got there. It's believed there was an explosion because debris was spread over the island. Luckily there was a snow squall just before mid-day which doused the flames somewhat. It prevented the professor's body from being burnt to a cinder. That's how the officers were able to determine that he'd been shot."

I shuddered involuntarily and thought of Sidorov and the gun he had used on me.

"Do you own a gun, Preston?" Geisler asked.

"I don't, but Sidorov had one. A forty-five automatic."

"Really. We believe it was a forty-five that was used on the professor."

I felt the first signs of panic rising in me, a tightening of the stomach muscles and a difficulty in forming words.

Geisler hobbled around to the front of me again and hovered like an expectant cat. "Now, why did you do it?"

I restrained a strong impulse to let him have a face full of knuckles and said, "I had nothing against Professor Brun. Therefore I had no reason to kill him."

"Somebody did."

"Then I suggest you start looking for whoever that is instead of wasting your time with me."

"But you were there when it happened," Geisler said. "How do you explain that?"

"I can't – unless it happened after we left the island."

"That's unlikely. The team arrived shortly after you flew out of there."

It seemed hopeless. I was in a vice that was closing fast. I leaned forward and buried my face in my sweaty palms, trying to think clearly through the haze that was clouding my mind.

"Feel like telling the truth now?" Geisler said, in a lower, gentler voice that belied his angry gaze.

"I have been telling the truth," I said.

So then they made me go over it again, and they listened intently, half expecting some variation on what I'd already told them and this only added to my edginess and made recollection of the facts all the more difficult. They fired more questions, pulled my story apart and examined it bit by bit with a sceptical eye. After a while even I was beginning to think there was no truth in it.

Eventually Kjarvel ended the interrogation by getting to his feet. He stared down at me, the bags under his eyes showing just how tired he was.

"That'll be all for now," he said. "I suggest you get some sleep. You've a long day ahead of you."

"I'm being held?"

"Of course you are. We need to make further inquiries. And don't worry – we'll talk to the people in Tasiilaq. Once we know what they have to say we'll speak again."

He pressed a button which brought in two uniforms and they dumped me back in the cell.

*

I imagine it was around seven when they came for me. I couldn't be sure of the time because my watch had stopped the night before and I hadn't noticed. I was hauled back up to Kjarvel's office where the same two were behind the desk looking not unlike a pair of dead-pan magistrates.

"Sit down, Mr Preston," Kjarvel said, and I took the continued use of the mister as a sign that he at least was not entirely convinced of my guilt.

The chair was in the same place and it was just as hard. When the officers had made themselves scarce, Kjarvel said, "You're going on a trip."

"How nice."

He ignored the sarcasm. "For some reason the Americans have expressed an interest in this affair and they want a word with you over at the embassy."

"The Americans! What the bloody hell has this got to do with them?"

"All I know is that until they've spoken to you about it we're not able to question you further or formally charge you."

"Supposing I refuse to see them?"

"You're in no position to refuse anything," Kjarvel made clear.

"So when do I go?"

"Immediately. Inspector Geisler will be going with you."

"That's reassuring." Something occurred to me then that I'd completely forgotten. I said quickly, "Hey, I think maybe Sidorov did get an opportunity to use the gun up at the station."

"Go on," Kjarvel said, leaning forward.

"Well, when we left the cabin the professor was still alive. What I forgot to mention was that Sidorov went back there."

"Alone?"

"Yeah. The woman said she'd left her gloves in the cabin. Sidorov offered to get them. She and I waited at the plane."

"Did you hear any shots?"

"No, but I had my head phones on by then."

Kjarvel nodded. "I suggest you explain that to the Americans.

Five minutes later I was bundled into the back of a police car. A constable got in beside me and Geisler sat up front with the driver. It wasn't a nice day. The sun had been swallowed by low choppy clouds and it looked very much like we were in for some rain. I felt especially cold without a coat, but nobody but me seemed particularly bothered about it.

The driver started her up and we moved into the stream of traffic flowing along the Posthusstraeti. We must have been in a hurry from the way the driver went about it, weaving in and out of the traffic with an audacity that only a police car could have got away with. We turned into the Austuratraeti and some way along it a dark blue Mercedes slipped into position in front of us. I only noticed it because I had nothing better to do than watch the traffic.

As we came to a junction opposite the Cabinet offices the driver of the Mercedes hesitated. First he indicated left, then changed his mind to go right. He crawled around the corner and we followed a few yards behind. By now the police driver was sufficiently annoyed to switch on the siren briefly and make threatening gestures through the windscreen.

But the driver of the Mercedes took not the blindest bit of notice and did not increase his speed beyond about ten mph. And then, for no apparent reason, the Mercedes screeched to a halt. The police driver slammed on his brakes and we were all thrown forward. The two cars were bumper to bumper.

Fuming, our driver turned to Geisler, saying, "I'll go see what's wrong."

As he opened the door to get out another voice demanded. "Stay as you are."

*

Through the open door there appeared a hand and it was clutching a revolver. In the same instant the back door next to me was wrenched open and another gun was shoved in.

"Okay, Preston. Out." The voice was loud and incisive. The face that dropped into view was hard and menacing. I experienced a cold spot of dread in my gut.

"What is this?" Geisler cried out.

But the man with his gun on me told Geisler to shut up and Geisler did. I didn't blame him. This character looked as if he knew how to use the toy he was holding and I didn't doubt that he would.

Slowly, cautiously, I shoved myself along the seat and got out of the car. The gunman kicked the door shut and I heard another muffled protest from Geisler before I found myself being prodded none too gently towards the Mercedes.

There was already a line of cars behind us and the irate motorists were pressing on their horns making enough noise to wake the dead. But it was all happening so fast we were probably the only ones aware of what was going on. The gunman had his back to the line of traffic and unfortunately for me there were no cars coming the other way and no pedestrians about.

A back door was flung open and I was pushed into the Mercedes. The gunman climbed in beside me and his friend opened the front door and slid in next to the driver. The engine had been left running and we pulled away with a screech of tyres that would not have disgraced a grand prix starting line.

The Mercedes swung around the first corner almost on two wheels. Then came the ear-splitting crash of misplaced gears before the car was screaming along a straight road.

With the gun still on me I dared to look through the rear window to see how far back Geisler was. But the police car was not to be seen. A bunch of keys was dropped into my lap.

"They will not go far without these."

I turned to look at him, head and shoulders above me. His face wasn't familiar and it wasn't the sort of face you'd ever be likely to forget; thick iron jawline, close-cropped hair and a head that greatly resembled the shape of a bullet.

After a while I felt the car slowing and glanced out the window. We had turned into a narrow, cobbled street behind some large warehouses. I gathered, from the gulls that wheeled and dived overhead, that we were somewhere near the waterfront. Several lorries were parked in the road, but there were no people about. The driver stopped the car and I was told to get out.

The fresh salty fragrance of the sea and the even stronger smell of dead fish was immediately apparent. With one of them holding each of my arms the other led the way to an orange Beetle Volkswagen parked across the road. On reaching the Volkswagen, Bullet Head ground the muzzle of his gun into the small of my back and told me to get in.

EIGHT

The Volkswagen carried us out of the city on one of the main roads through the suburbs. We ran for a couple of miles through green rippling fields and then started to skirt the base of a mountain along a winding road.

I began to have visions of being eliminated in some gruesome fashion — my body trussed up, weighted down and dropped into a lake. A coldness was clutching at my insides and the butterflies were dancing around like crazy.

Gradually the road withered away until it was merely a strip made of volcanic cinders and stones.

It began to rain, slowly at first in large aggressive droplets that splattered harshly on the windscreen.

The driver and his front seat passenger were both huge and were probably lying in the same dirt track when an elephant trampled on their faces. Who they hell were they? And whatever did they want with me? For that matter why was everyone so anxious to get their hands on me?

Even the Americans were in on the act and that, surely, said something for my importance. But why was I important? What did I know or what did they think I knew that made me such a target? I thought about it as we continued through the rain. Now and then lightning flickered in the pall of grey, wind-driven clouds.

Suddenly Bullet Head leaned forward and placed a hand on the driver's shoulder. "Pull over. This is the place."

For the first time I realized he was not Icelandic. His accent had too much of a drawl to it and I judged it to be of Slavic origin. The other two, who had spoken to one another briefly in broken English during the drive, had also revealed themselves as not being indigenous to the country. Czechs? Poles? Or Russians maybe?

It was difficult to see much with the rain gushing down with such vengeance, but I was able to make out a small corrugated hut set back a little from the road. The car jolted to a standstill and the driver rubbed a hole in the condensation that had gathered on the window and peered out.

"He isn't here yet," he said. "What time is it?"

Bullet Head told him it was almost eight, adding, "He'll be along soon. We can wait inside."

I was ordered out of the car at gunpoint and then man-handled towards the hut across some stony ground that crunched under our feet. I tried to see beyond the hut, but the curtain of rain made that impossible. It was coming down in profusion and in that short walk from the car my clothes got soaked through.

One of the men ran ahead and opened the door and we all trampled in. I stood there, shaking off the rain as the door slammed shut behind me. In that single chilling moment I was gripped by a sudden fear that gave rise to a feeling of nausea inside me.

71

The three of them were standing close to me. I could even smell them. A more formidable trio you couldn't imagine. I cursed my own rotten luck for finding myself completely at their mercy.

These huts were all over Iceland, set up at the tourist attractions for the convenience of sightseers on such days as this. The inside consisted of a wooden bench and nothing else. There was a poor excuse for a window, the glass so dirty you couldn't see through it. We were in semi-darkness.

"What happens now?" I said, fear creeping into my voice.

The big man with the Bullet Head gestured for me to sit down.

"We wait," he said.

I went and sat on the bench. Behind me the rain sprayed noisily against the window. A heavy, nauseous chill ran through me.

"Police put you through it, did they?" he asked, a crooked smile tugging at the sides of his mouth.

I didn't answer. I didn't know what to say. He came and sat down beside me while the other two shuffled around the room taking turns to look outside. I could smell his minty breath.

"I wanted to be a pilot when I was a boy," he said. "But I never got the chance. Seems like a glam job."

He was looking at me, his hard eyes like chunks of glass, his mouth flat and narrow.

"Shame about your plane," he said. "Those babies are not cheap."

I willed myself to remain calm. *Don't panic. Don't give him a reason to become violent. Try to think of a way out of this.*

But it was hard to just sit there. My chest hurt. It was tight and burning and I was struggling to catch my breath.

"What do you want?" I asked after a couple of seconds. I tried to make it sound like I wasn't scared when really I was on the verge of shaking myself into a fit.

"Be patient," he said, in a low, hoarse voice.

Then he leaned back against the wall with all the grace of a drunken seaman. He produced a stick of gum from his jacket pocket and stuffed it gingerly into his mouth. He didn't only look like a pig, he ate like one, making more noise than would have been necessary had he been eating from a bag of crisps.

The man whose turn it was to look outside called back over his shoulder. "He's here, Otto."

Bullet Head responded by jumping to his feet so I assumed he was Otto. He rushed over to the door and I heard a car draw to a stop on the gravel outside.

I stared at the door. Rain splashed into the hut on a fierce wind that brought the cold in also. Footsteps sounded on the gravel outside, grew louder as the visitor approached.

Then he entered.

I know the medical profession would say it's impossible, but I'd swear my heart stopped when I saw who it was. At first he busied himself with his ski coat collar, folding it down and cursing loudly as rain trickled onto his neck. Then he looked at me and his face became distorted in a wide, virulent smile.

Sidorov said, "I was hoping we'd meet again."

As he came at me his eyes lit up with fury. I braced myself. The first blow caught me on the left temple and the back of his hand all but knocked my head off. The second blow was even harder, or maybe it just seemed that way because the mouth is a more sensitive area. I could taste blood and a quick probe with my tongue told me that the inside of my bottom lip had been slashed on a tooth.

Having got whatever it was off his chest Sidorov stood there staring down at me, his face suffused with anger and his lips set in a vulpine smile.

"You will not be so lucky a second time, Preston."

He slapped me again. The palm of his hand must have left a big red mark on my cheek because the pain was abominable.

I said desperately, "Look, what am I supposed to have done for Christ's sake?"

The hand came down again, but this time I raised my arm to block it and kicked out at his groin. I'm not an expert at such things so it came as no great surprise when I shoved my shoe into his right thigh instead. He groaned, stumbled back and by that time Otto and one of the others had both my arms pinned back against the wall.

"That was foolish," Sidorov said, rubbing the shoe stain from his trousers. He turned to Otto. "Has he said anything?"

Otto shook his head.

"Very well, Preston," Sidorov said. "I want to know exactly what you told the police? And for your own sake dispense with the smart answers."

I swallowed. Coughed. Hacked up saliva. Prickles of fear rippled across my skin.

Sidorov glared at me with a demented gleam in his eyes.

"Speak to me or so help me I will hurt you bad," he raged.

"I told them everything," I said. "What do you think? And they told me what you did to the professor."

"And they suspect you?" The idea apparently amused him because he grinned. It was not a pleasant sight.

"Why did you do it?" I asked.

"It's of no consequence."

"You bastard."

As if he hadn't heard me, he said, "What did you tell the police about the corpse?"

So it *was* the corpse he was interested in. The man whose name was believed to be Maxwell. My mind flashed back to their reaction after the tarpaulin was pulled back. They had expressed no emotion, no sense of relief. I should have realized then that their story about the company plane was at best a little dubious.

"Well, Preston," Sidorov said, a frown drawing fresh lines across his face.

"I told them exactly what happened," I said.

He wasn't satisfied.

"Go on."

"That's it. I said that you and the woman couldn't identify the guy. So we thanked the professor and left there."

I glanced quickly at the door, but any hopes of making a run for it were dashed because the other of the three gorillas who had brought me here had his back against it.

"Did you tell them about the watch?" Sidorov asked.

For the moment I couldn't see the significance of the watch, but then it hit me. The inscription.

"Yes, I told them," I said. "Why wouldn't I?"

"Did you mention the inscription?"

I nodded. "Of course I did."

He pulled his lips back across his teeth and said, "I should have shot you instead of leaving you to burn."

I think he intended to rain a few more blows on me then, but a noise outside stopped him. Otto let go of my arm, moved swiftly to the door and looked out. A moment later he announced, "It's a coach. Tourists."

Sidorov began to size up the situation, but I doubt that thinking came easily to him despite the size of his head.

"What is happening now?" he said after a moment.

Otto looked again. "They've stopped. Now they're getting off and most of them are heading towards the crater."

So we were near a crater. There are lots of them in Iceland, dotted about the wide volcanic zones and they are always a favourite with the tourists, whatever the conditions.

Sidorov turned on me, his eyes full of menace. "To your feet. We're leaving here. One wrong move and I'll shoot you. Remember that."

The door was pulled open and we paraded out. The coach was a long red monster parked on the other side of the road from the two cars. Sidorov had a Mini that he'd left alongside the Volkswagen.

Most of the tourists had already stepped down from the coach and were branching off in every direction under big colourful umbrellas.

A small group of indeterminate Europeans was walking towards the hut and as we passed them a teenage girl smiled at me. I did hope she'd notice what was going on and raise the alarm, but Otto was careful to conceal the gun.

We reached the Volkswagen and Sidorov went around to his own car. The door was wrenched open and Otto applied pressure on the gun. I acted quickly then, knowing full well I'd get no more chances. I diverted the gun with my elbow and slammed a fist into his surprised face. I don't think it hurt him much — though it hurt me like hell — but it did cause him to lose his balance which was more than I could have hoped for.

He tumbled awkwardly to the ground, dropping the gun. In the split second after I had only one of them to contend with, the other having gone around the driver's side. As he came at me I placed both hands on the door and swung it viciously outwards. He was a big enough target and it was a big enough door. He let out a painful grunt as it slammed into him and he staggered backwards.

I turned and legged it towards the coach. The car had screened the incident from the tourists so nobody was paying me any attention. I thought at first of seeking help among them, but they were mostly kids, so I decided not to get them involved. Instead, I ran past the coach and into the rain.

*

I came to the crater where most of the tourists had gathered under a ceiling of umbrellas. I veered to the right and followed the rim. It was the usual thing, a huge hole in the ground with sloping sides and a pool of rain water at the bottom. This particular one was about two hundred feet across.

I saw a wooden sign up ahead, but before reaching it I changed course and scrambled down a steep hill. At the bottom I continued running with the rain rushing at me like a hail of bullets. Beneath me the ground was a dull, scorched yellow and it crumbled under my feet like freshly baked cake.

All around the rain began to unfold strange crater-shaped holes filled with bubbling blue mud. Some of the holes were so small as not to be noticed, but others were deep gurgling pools many yards across. It was like crossing a vast lunar landscape.

78

I realized suddenly that I was on a sulphur field. I should have known it the moment I stepped onto the scorched earth. At some time, probably in the mid-19th century, sulphur had been extracted here. Which meant that the mud in the holes was not only thick and deep, but also boiling. The sign I'd managed to miss had probably warned of the dangers of stepping onto it. And the dangers are real, for the holes are forming all the time and you can quite easily tread onto what you think is solid ground and have it open up under you.

"There he is," someone shouted.

Two figures appeared out of nowhere about seventy feet back. I broke into a run again, mindful now of the added danger. But the two men were gaining on me, seemingly finding it much easier to wend their way among the holes.

They trampled indiscriminately over ground that I had crossed so hesitantly only seconds before. Maybe, I thought hopefully, they were not aware of the danger underfoot.

Soon the rain was no longer stinging my face because my flesh was without feeling, numbed by a thousand pointed darts flung at me with a tremendous force. After a while I was disregarding caution myself, running with the same recklessness as my pursuers.

Suddenly, above the roar of wind and rain, I heard a shot. I knew they were well within range, but I couldn't even hazard a guess as to where the bullet went. I looked back over my shoulder, which was a stupid thing to do because it caused me to lose my footing and fall over.

I came down on my face only inches from a hole brimming with that ubiquitous blue mud. I scrambled onto all fours before looking back. I couldn't see them, but that was only because visibility had shrunk to a mere thirty or so feet as the rain increased its load and kicked up a thickening mist of ground spray.

I didn't think it would be long before they came and I was right. They emerged through the grey wall side by side, guns out in front. They were no longer running, for having lost sight of their prey they were forced to search their flanks through narrowed eyes.

It was the taller of the two, Otto I think, who saw me first. He yelled to his pal and gestured towards me with the gun. The ground exploded around me and one bullet whistled right under my nose.

But I managed to keep on my feet and in one piece. To say they were not very good marksmen would be a polite way of saying that any ten-year-old with average vision could have done better. Not that I was complaining. It gave me the precious few seconds I needed to put distance between us.

A long time seemed to pass during which the wild chase continued and eventually it was taking all my strength just to stay upright.

Finally I had to stop to catch my breath. I didn't see them when I turned round. I waited and watched for them to appear as before. But they never came. I stood for about ten minutes, silent save for my own heavy breathing.

Then I went back the way I'd come, thinking that maybe they had lost me and were searching either to the right or left where I couldn't see them through the rain. I knew well enough that if I continued going away from the crater I'd be going into an unknown world from which I might never return. I walked on. It took an eternity to cover twenty yards. I was being more careful now, testing the ground before every step.

Then something caught my eye and I moved towards it. I knelt beside one of the larger holes. The mud in it was bubbling like crazy. A gun was lying near the edge. At once I realized what had happened, could even imagine him falling, unable to call out as the boiling, broiling mud overcame him.

Clearly this hole had only just been formed which was why there was so much commotion on the surface. I looked at the thick blue mud, pimpled with gas bubbles and chunks of clay. It would be a horrible way to die, but I felt no pity for whoever was down there.

I picked up the gun and headed back towards the crater.

*

There was no sign of Otto. I wondered if he was the one who had perished in the hole. I saw Sidorov standing at the edge of the crater with one of the other men. They were both looking in the direction we had run.

The sightseers were still milling around and some of them seemed to be aware that something untoward was going on. They were looking about anxiously as if expecting something to happen.

I was watching it all from the other side of the crater, my head just above the rim. Up here the rain had let up some and visibility was much better. I lowered myself back down the slope and circled the crater. Sidorov was to my right and the cars and hut just ahead across the road.

I waited until they were both looking the other way, then, keeping low, darted across the road to the Mini. I looked inside, saw the key had been left in the ignition. I eased the door open and removed it. Then I crawled over to the Volkswagen and my run of luck continued when I discovered the ignition key to this car had also been left in place. I jumped in and started her up.

The Volkswagen pulled away with a roar of acceleration. As I jerked her onto the road I looked back and saw Sidorov reach inside his overcoat. But before he could pull his weapon from his pocket I was already swerving the other way and piling on the speed.

NINE

By the time I got back to Reykjavik I'd already convinced myself that going to the police would achieve nothing. They were probably convinced now that I was in cahoots with the guys who had hijacked the car. So I decided that a certain amount of initiative was now called for. I had to make an effort myself to find out what was going on.

And I knew just where to start.

It was noon when I parked the Volkswagen on the road that skirts the harbour. I still had the gun I'd found beside the sulphur pit so I pushed it into the waistband of my trousers and covered it with the sweater.

The quay was crowded with ships of all nationalities being loaded and unloaded. And it was noisy. The loud moan of mechanical cranes. The shrill cry of the gulls. Further down there were dozens of fishing boats. Sail-ropes festooned the air from a forest of masts and colourful hulls bobbed aimlessly in their own reflections.

It was good to see the place bustling again. It had taken years for the city, and indeed for the country, to get back on its feet after the collapse of the banking system in 2008. Now there was a new economic model in place – one that focused on exploiting Iceland's wealth of natural resources, which included increasing its fishing quotas in the North Atlantic.

I had set out with the intention of spotting the *Hekla* among all those trawlers, but it didn't take me long to realize it wasn't going to be easy. There were so many of them and not all the names could be seen. I spent a fruitless half hour trudging up and down the quay getting wetter and more downhearted.

Then I asked an old fisherman if he knew where the *Hekla* was berthed. He said no but suggested I try at the harbourmaster's office. I soon found the office and in less than ten minutes I knew that the *Hekla* was a converted fishing boat that her owner chartered out to tourists.

It didn't take me long to find her. She was moored among a line of old pleasure craft. One look told me she was the boat I'd seen in the bay. I suddenly felt warm with excitement despite the fact that I was soaked to the skin.

She was a forty-foot job with more wrinkles than a stale prune. It was obvious she wasn't in a fit state any more for standing up to battering seas and gale force winds out in the cod grounds, but she was functional and ideal for coastal pleasure trips.

I felt it safe to assume that none of Sidorov's cronies were around so I ventured on board. The deck was about four feet below the quay and I lowered myself down an iron ladder to get to it. The deck was wet and slippery and I walked slowly, cat-like, trying not to make a sound.

I peered through the wheelhouse window, saw it was empty and very gently slid back the door and looked in. There was the usual paraphernalia inside; charts, navigational instruments, a couple of coffee mugs.

I left the wheelhouse and went forward to the hatch, then lowered myself into the semi-darkness of the cabin area. There were two tiny cabins and they were empty.

I went back to the wheelhouse. To my great delight I found an anorak hanging from a hook behind the door. My goose pimples jumped for joy as I snatched it down and slipped into it. I pulled the zip right up to the neck and put the gun into one of the pockets.

I searched the wheelhouse assiduously, but found nothing which served to show that Gudren and Sidorov had been on board. I pulled open a drawer and rifled through some papers and charts. They told me only that the boat was owned by a bloke named Eirnerson. There was also some loose kronur in the drawer and as the police had all my loot I helped myself to it.

I couldn't think what to do then, other than wait and see who turned up. There was no point going to the police because I'd found nothing so far that could help me in any way.

I sat on the helmsman's stool and leaned against the bulkhead. Through the window I had a clear view of the quay and I'd be able to see anyone approaching. An hour passed and I began to doze. It was only the unsuitability of my precarious perch that prevented me from dropping off altogether. My clothes had almost dried but I felt worse than ever. The pain at the back of my head, which I hadn't noticed during all the morning's excitement, was back and becoming increasingly unbearable. My chest was hurting as well and I was wishing to God I was back in the hospital with that pretty nurse bestowing pity on me.

Another half an hour and I was about ready to leave the boat and enquire among the fishermen about the owner's whereabouts, when a man I'd been watching walk along the quay stopped above the *Hekla*. I slid quickly off the stool and crouched low in the belly of the wheelhouse, raising my head to see through the window.

The man was about fifty, dressed in reefer jacket and gumboots. He stood there looking down at the boat and I thought for one horrible moment he'd seen me. But then he began to lower himself onto the deck.

Suddenly I wasn't cold anymore and I broke out in a sweat. I took out the gun with a shaking hand and stopped breathing.

The man reached the wheelhouse and the door started to slide back. I got a grip of myself, sprang to my feet and jerked it open all the way.

The man jumped back, a fearful look on his lean, unshaven face. His eyes dropped to the gun rattling in my hand.

"Come in," I demanded in a low voice.

He didn't move and I wondered if he understood English. So I repeated the command more loudly and this time he stepped forward.

"Now close the door."

He clearly understood everything I was saying. Without turning he reached a hand behind him and closed the door.

"Who are you?" I asked.

"I . . . I own this boat," he stammered.

"So you're Eirnerson?"

He nodded.

I glanced out the window. "You alone?"

He nodded again. "Look, if it's money you want..."

"I don't want your money. I'm here to ask you some questions. Now raise your arms."

He lifted them above his head and I stepped forward and frisked him quickly with my free hand.

"What are you doing here?" I said, stepping back.

"I've come to prepare my boat. Some people are taking her out tomorrow."

I decided to get right to the crux of the matter and said, "Who took this boat out yesterday?"

Something happened to his eyes that telegraphed the fact that he was going to tell a lie.

"N... nobody had her yesterday," he said. "She was here all day."

"You're lying."

"It's the truth."

"It's what you told the police, but it isn't the truth. I happen to know that this tub was out in the bay yesterday afternoon."

"You are mistaken."

I shrugged. "Okay, lie down."

"Huh?"

I raised the gun.

"I said, lie down."

He needed no more prompting. He dropped to his knees and stretched out on his back, staring up at me.

"Now try again. Who were they?"

He splattered something quite unintelligible and dribbled all over the floor.

"Who are you?" he said.

I shook my head. "Never mind who I am. I'll ask one more time and if you don't tell me what I want to know, so help me, I'll shoot you."

That did it. He said, "They came yesterday morning. Two men. They wanted to hire the boat for the afternoon. Please, take the gun away from my face."

"Was there a woman with them when they returned?"

"Yes, and also another man. A big man."

"Why did you lie to the police about it?"

"I was afraid."

"Why? Did you know these people?"

"No, but they threatened me. They said they would kill me if I told anyone. And they gave me money."

So I'd been right about one thing. Sidorov had intended to kill me long before we arrived in Iceland. They must have contacted their friends either from the research station or from Tasiilaq.

"Where can I find them?"

"I don't know?"

I pressed the gun against his nostrils and let him smell the thing. "Try again."

"I swear I know nothing. You should try one of the drivers."

"Who?"

"Taxi drivers. Up there at the rank."

"You saw them get in a taxi?"

"No, but they asked me where they could find one. I got the impression they had only one car between them and wanted to go to separate locations."

I stood up and kicked his arm. "OK, on your feet."

He scrambled up and stood with his back against the door, his gaze on the gun.

"What are you going to do?" he asked.

"I should shoot you," I told him. "You've given me plenty of trouble."

"But I didn't dare talk. I was afraid. I have a family."

"Well for your information these people are dangerous. They're murderers and they've been trying to kill me. So the police will want to talk to you again."

"Am I in trouble?"

"Not if you come clean and explain why you lied first time around."

I gave him Kjarvel's name and told him to call the cops when I'd gone.

"You can tell them I came to see you," I said, putting the gun back in my pocket. "And for your sake don't lie about anything. Got that?"

He nodded. "For sure."

I found the taxi rank easily enough. About six of them formed a line outside a row of shops. I started at the back of the line and worked my way to the front, asking each driver if he remembered Sidorov's party. Fortunately most

Icelandic cabbies speak English so I didn't get a lot of blank faces in response to my questions.

It was the second driver from the front who told me what I wanted to know. He'd taken a man and a young woman to a house in the suburbs the previous afternoon. I ducked into the back and told him to take me there.

TEN

The house was a detached, two storey affair in a quiet
residential area near Laugardalur Park. It was situated on a
corner, fronted by a neat lawn with a garden at the back
surrounded by a high wooden fence.

I told the driver to pass it and park up the road. When
we stopped I asked him to wait. I glanced through the back
window at the house. There were no cars outside, but that
didn't mean there wasn't anyone at home. The lawn offered
no cover as there was only a two-foot high wall around it.

The houses in the street were spread about fifteen yards
apart and between the corner house and its nearest
neighbour there was a hedge and two adjoining garages.

I got out and walked casually towards the house,
stopping outside the front gate of the one before it. I opened
the gate and moved swiftly up the drive. Fortunately it
didn't seem as if this house was occupied.

At the head of the drive I followed a path that led
between the garage and the side of the house. There was a
door in the garage wall set in a recess and the side door to
the house was directly opposite.

The wall of the house ended first and the back garden
opened out in front of me. I edged out slowly and hurried
across the back garden to the rear of the garage. There I
was on a section of lawn which had been dug up and paved

over. A drainpipe ran up the wall of the garage about a foot out from the hedge.

Climbing drainpipes isn't one of my specialities so I didn't find it easy. But with perseverance I managed to grab the flat roof of the garage and pull myself up so that I could see into the garden of the end house.

It was much the same as the garden I was in only the entire area was grassed over.

The garage structure was semi-detached and by resting my feet lightly on the hedge and holding on to the roof I was able to work my way across and drop onto the soft damp grass. When I was reasonably sure nobody had seen me I sneaked out from behind the garage and up to the back of the house.

Soon I was on the path between the garage and the house. I came to the side door of the house. Just then I heard a car on the road in front of the house.

I jumped back and dashed the few yards to the recess in the garage wall. I flattened myself against the door as the car drove up to the house and the engine was switched off.

I leaned forward slightly and had a look. The car was Sidorov's Mini. A second later the Russian and the other man who had watched me drive away from the crater climbed out.

I groped behind me for the door knob and turned it. The door opened inwards and I stumbled into the gloom of the garage. Just at that moment the kitchen door opened and a woman's voice said in English, "What has happened?" I recognized it at once as Gudren's voice.

"He got away," I heard Sidorov tell her.

"You fools."

Only when the door shut did I start to breathe again. I waited a few minutes, then stepped out of the garage and crept along the path to the drive, stopping next to Sidorov's Mini.

I looked inside for an ignition key and when I didn't see one I assumed they had started it by some other means or had managed to get a key which this time Sidorov had pocketed. I reached for the bonnet release and lifted it up. Then I ripped out the plug leads.

Within seconds I was tearing out of the front gate. I looked back at the house, but there was nobody at any of the windows. When I reached the taxi I climbed in.

"Do you have a mobile phone?" I asked the driver.

He nodded. "Of course. Is there a problem?"

"I need to use it to call the police."

Thirty seconds later I was through to the Central Police Station. I gave my name and asked to be put through to Kjarvel. When he came on the line, he said, "Preston? Where the hell are you?"

"You've got to listen to me," I said.

"Just tell me where you are."

"Hold your horses and listen. I've found Sidorov and the woman."

A long pause, then, "Where?"

"At a house in the suburbs."

"Are you alone?"

"Yes, except for the taxi driver who brought me here. Get over here quickly before they leave."

"The address?"

I gave it to him and waited for him to jot it down.

"I'll have to contact Inspector Geisler," he said. "He'll want to be there."

"Do what you like, but for Christ's sake hurry up."

*

The police got there twenty minutes later. Three cars. There was a screech of tyres, then a mass of uniforms materialized and converged on the house, stamping across the lawn about as delicately as a herd of elephants. I waited in the taxi for a few minutes so that if there was any shooting I wouldn't be caught up in it.

Meanwhile a long black American job arrived on the scene and disgorged three men. One was Geisler, wearing a worried expression. He rushed straight over to the house. I bade the bemused cabbie a fond farewell and crossed the road.

When I reached the front gate Geisler and his two cocky companions emerged from the house. Geisler saw me, raised his eyebrows and limped over.

When he reached me he wiped the smile right off my face. "So where are they?" he said.

I looked at the house and then at the impotent Mini.

"Come on, Preston. What is this, more games?"

"I saw them inside not more than twenty minutes ago," I said.

"The house is empty."

I pointed to the Mini. "Look, I even put their car out of commission."

"Did they see you?"

"No."

Another car drew up. Kjarvel stepped from it and came bounding over.

"Well," he said. "Have you got them?"

Geisler looked at me. "Are you going to tell him or shall I?"

"They've gone," I said simply.

Kjarvel stared at me, lips tight across his teeth. "How?"

I shrugged. "I swiped the plug leads from their car before phoning you so they must have left on foot."

"Are you sure they didn't have another car?"

I pointed along the road. "I was sitting in the taxi the whole time. Nobody came out of the house. I've seen no other cars."

"So they must have gone out the back."

"I guess so."

Kjarvel and Geisler ran into the house and I followed. It soon became evident what had happened. The back door was open and so too was the garden gate which led to another minor road with houses and cars.

"We'll get a search underway," Kjarvel said. "But if they're in a car they could be several miles away by now."

Then he turned to me, adding, "You've got a lot of explaining to do, Preston."

I issued a heavy sigh. "Now why doesn't that surprise me?"

ELEVEN

Geisler's two taciturn companions turned out to be from the American embassy. They sat on either side of me in that big black monster of a car while Geisler sat up front with the driver.

I was whisked to the embassy in faster time than it takes to open a tin of beans and not a word was spoken by anyone.

The American embassy is in downtown Reykjavik, a large but unimposing building on the Laufasvegur. My escort led me into the building through the main entrance. A private lift took us up several floors so quietly I wasn't aware we'd moved until I stepped out into another corridor. Through a window I saw the roofs of the city, wet and shimmering under a grey sky.

We arrived at an unmarked door, and the embassy blokes told Geisler and me to wait inside.

It was an office and quite the most comfortable place of work I had ever seen. It was full of red leather and varnished wood with a thick shag-pile carpet that made standing a sheer pleasure. A big antique desk stood proudly beneath a narrow window that overlooked the street.

A portrait of George Washington hung on one wall and his stern face scowled across the room at a large crinkled map of Iceland and Greenland which had been pinned not-quite-straight to the wall opposite.

Geisler made himself at home in one of the armchairs, one leg crossed over the other, and took out his cigarettes.

"You don't smoke, do you?"

"I can do without the chit-chat, Inspector," I said. "Why have I been brought here?"

"You'll soon be told."

"I want to know now. I've had just about enough of being pushed around."

He lit a cigarette. "Just sit down, Preston, and be patient."

I felt the temper come up in me, but it was checked when the door opened and three men came in. One was Kjarvel, the other two I didn't know. They were both clean shaven and impeccably dressed: typical embassy Johns right down to their highly-polished shoes and knife-sharp trouser creases.

One of them came straight over to me and smiled. "I'm Howard Dean. This is my assistant Roy Bridges. Mr Kjarvel of the Icelandic police you already know."

I liked Dean instantly, probably because he was the first person in two days who didn't look at me as if I was the worst thing since the Yorkshire Ripper. He had a benign smile that suited his round jolly face and a pot belly that hinted at either contentment or gluttony. About forty to forty-five I'd have said.

Bridges was sickeningly handsome; in fact he might have stepped right out of one of those glossy film star magazines. He was about my age, but taller and more athletically built than I could ever hope to be. His hair was jet black and it curled slightly around the ears.

"Won't you sit down, gentlemen," Dean said. "There are plenty of chairs."

We all sat down, Dean in the chair behind the desk. Without saying anything he took a thin black wallet from his pocket and passed it to me.

"I suggest you check this out," he said.

I flipped it open. There wasn't much to it, a few printed words, a cut-out picture of Dean that rather did him justice and an official looking government stamp. It failed to explain why the CIA were sticking their noses in this.

I tossed it back to him. "I'm no spy."

He laughed. "Glad to hear it. Would you like something to eat or drink while we talk?"

"I wouldn't say no to a cup of tea. No sugar."

Dean asked the others what they wanted, then gave the order to his secretary through the intercom on his desk.

He looked up. "It'll be in shortly. Meanwhile I suggest we get on with it." Turning his gaze directly on me, he added, "I suppose you're wondering what this is all about."

"It had crossed my mind."

He grinned. "Well we'd like to know more about that corpse the Inuits took to the research station."

"All I know about that is what I've already told the police."

"We'll see," he said. "First I'd like to ease your mind some by saying that we're pretty sure you did not murder the professor."

Which was certainly a turn for the books. I said, "I only wish the police shared that view."

"We do." This was Geisler. "We spoke to Bill Osborn and Else Jensen in Tasiilaq. They confirmed what you told us. And our American friends have provided further evidence to support your version of events."

It was like a heavy weight had been lifted from my shoulders.

"So you can relax on that score, Mr Preston," Dean said. "But we do want to know more about that corpse. Maybe you can help us, maybe not. Somebody else obviously thinks you can."

"Somebody else?"

He nodded. "The guys who kidnapped you this morning. Somehow they found out you were coming here. They obviously didn't want you to speak to us."

"It was Sidorov," I said.

"And I gather you traced him to this house in the suburbs."

"That's right."

"Might I ask how?"

I told him about the *Hekla*, Eirnerson and the taxi driver.

"And you've no idea how they knew the house was about to be raided?"

"That's about it. I'm pretty sure they didn't see me."

Dean thought about it. "So what happened after they snatched you from the police car?"

I told him about my trip to the volcano where Sidorov admitted killing the professor. He raised his brow when I said that one of Sidorov's henchmen must have fallen into the sulphur pit.

"Did Sidorov say why he killed Brun?" Dean asked.

"No, but he did want to know what I'd told the police about the inscription on the watch."

Dean leaned forward on his desk. "I was going to come to the watch next. Did you see this inscription yourself?"

"Sure. I was the one who took it off the dead man's wrist. I thought it was worth checking."

"And tell me what the inscription said."

I shrugged. "To Maxwell from Jean. And there were a couple of crosses."

"You're absolutely sure of this?"

"Of course I am. It's an easy thing to remember."

"OK, now you told the police that the professor was sure the man had only been dead a day or two. Is that right?"

"That's what he said and I tended to agree with him. I'm pretty sure if the body had been in the water longer than that it would have been in a much worse condition. That's why I thought it unlikely that the dead man had been on board the plane that crashed five days ago."

"You mean the plane that was supposedly owned by the fictitious company called Polar Invesments."

"Exactly."

There was a knock at the door and Dean's secretary brought in the refreshments he'd ordered. While she poured the hot drinks the conversation lapsed into idle chatter about the latest wrangle between Iceland and the rest of

Europe over fishing limits. Her chore done, she hurried out of the room.

I said, "Did you know this bloke, Maxwell?"

Dean glanced briefly at Bridges before answering. "We knew him."

"Then who…?"

Dean raised his hand to stop me. "Before you ask any questions in that direction there's something I'd like you to look at."

He reached inside his desk drawer and pulled out a thick buff folder.

"Take a look at these photographs. Tell me if any of the characters who've been trying to kill you are in there."

"So they're mug shots?"

"You could call them that."

He handed me the folder. The cover and the first page were blank. Beyond that each successive page contained two photographs of the same person. Beneath each photograph was a foreign sounding name and a six-figure number. Most of the photographs had clearly been taken from a distance when the subject was unaware, but there were some facial close-ups.

I was halfway through the folder when I saw the name Vladamir Kolonov under two photographs of a man entering the National Museum in Reykjavik. He was wearing a dark brown leather coat and seemed totally unaware that his picture was being taken. I unclipped the page and handed it to Dean.

"This is Sidorov," I said.

Dean glanced at the photograph. "That just about confirms what we suspected," he said.

"Who is he?" Kjarvel asked.

Dean sat back. He kept us on the edges of our chairs as he picked up his cup and sipped coffee. Then, from the memory file inside his head, he said, "Vladamir Kolonov. We suspect he was born in Leningrad in sixty five, the son of a government official. He's known to have been in Reykjavik under assumed names on a number of occasions. He appears to be a fluent speaker of several languages including Icelandic." He paused and his eyes narrowed as he looked at me. "He's also known to us as a ruthless killer and one of the FSB's most active agents in the West."

I frowned. "What's the FSB?"

"It's the Federal Security Service of the Russian Federation," Dean said. "The agency that's responsible for counter-intelligence, border controls and counter terrorism. It's the successor to the notorious KGB."

My stomach fell apart. There's no other way to describe the sensation. It was as though every muscle inside me had broken in two like the strings of an overworked guitar.

The KGB. That dreaded secret police force that remained the stuff of nightmares. Murder. Torture. Kidnap. You name it and they were supposed to have done in as a matter of routine before the demise of the USSR in 1991.

"It must be quite a shock to you," Dean said.

That had to be the understatement of the century. I said, "What do you think?"

"I'd think myself lucky to be still alive."

And I did, so much so that I said a quick, silent prayer of thanks to whoever had been watching over me. Maybe it was Anna.

"You'll find him of course," I said. "Now that you know he killed Professor Brun and tried to kill me."

"I doubt it," Dean said. "By now he'll probably be on his way back to Moscow. The Kremlin will not be happy about what's happened. They'll want to know why he wasn't able to contain the problem and why you managed to get away."

He handed the page about Sidorov to Kjarvel. "Here. This is your department. I suggest the airports and docks. You never know, we might strike lucky, but I very much doubt it."

Kjarvel was up and out of the room in an instant.

Dean turned back to me. "Take another look. See if you can spot any more of them."

"Are they all with the FSB?" I asked.

He nodded. "They're people we suspect of being with them. Each of them has lived or has been seen in Iceland recently. If my memory serves me right then those photographs of Sidorov — or Kolonov — were taken about three months ago."

"If you knew he was an enemy agent why didn't you have him arrested?"

He grinned. "Because we can't go around arresting everybody we suspect of being Russian spies. The Cold War ended years ago and we're all supposed to be part of one big happy family. But as you would expect we do keep an eye on them."

I flicked through the pages in the folder with my thumb. "Seems as if Iceland is popular among the Russians."

"There are twenty-two to be exact."

"Why so many?"

"It isn't so many, considering the relative importance of Iceland."

"So what is so important about it?"

"Partly its position," he said. "Which is of great strategic importance, especially in time of war. This country stands in the middle of the North Atlantic. Russian ships out of Murmansk are very active in these waters and so are their subs. So we have to keep track of them."

I think he wanted to continue, but the intercom stopped him. He pressed the switch and his secretary said, "Colonel Matthews is here, sir."

"Good. Send him in." To me Dean said, "What about the rest of the folder."

I leafed through the photographs, but there were no more familiar faces. I wondered why Gudren wasn't among them.

The door opened suddenly and in walked a mountain of a man in US Navy attire. There was more muscle than fat beneath his immaculate uniform if his strong, wide jawline was anything to go by. The shoulders of his jacket looked as if they had been starched while stretched over a soccer goalmouth and I wondered if he really filled them.

"Hi there," he beamed to the room in general.

Dean rose to the occasion and held out his hand. The big man ambled over and shook it.

"Glad you could come, Colonel."

"My pleasure."

Dean introduced him to everyone, explaining that he was with the 821st Security Forces Squadron at the Thule Air Base in northern Greenland.

I knew a little about the base as did most people who lived in the region. It was located 750 miles below the Arctic Circle and had been there since the early fifties. Thule was America's most northerly facility and home to the 821st Air Base Group. It served as a crucial part of Nato's defence strategy and housed the Ballistic Missile Early Warning System. It's location had always been a major source of friction between Washington and Moscow.

The Colonel took a seat and listened attentively as Dean filled him in on what had happened.

"So we were right," the Colonel said, taking a chair. "They could be alive."

"Looks that way," Dean replied.

"I guess they're way out in front of us then, huh?"

Dean shook his head. "Not necessarily. The fact that they went to such trouble to catch Mr Preston must mean they're no nearer than we are."

"You think so?"

Dean nodded. "It seems to me they're still anxious to keep us out of it, which must mean they haven't come up with anything themselves yet."

"So where do we go from here?" the Colonel said.

"Any luck your end?"

The Colonel shrugged. "Since this morning when you contacted me the Icelandic Coast Guard have been on it. Their aircraft has been combing the area between Tasiilaq and Scoresbysund. We've also alerted the Danish navy and we ourselves have been monitoring satellite images of the Denmark Strait."

When Dean next spoke it was almost in a whisper, as if he were thinking aloud. "If only we knew exactly what we were looking for."

I decided that I'd had just about enough of being left in the dark and said sharply, "Would you prefer that I left the room or am I to be told what the bloody hell this is all about?"

I was suddenly the centre of attention again, but now I felt like an intruder.

Dean broke the silence. "I guess you deserve to know after what you've been through. Like some more tea? It'll take time to explain."

TWELVE

Dean rested his elbows on the desk and formed a steeple with his short stubby fingers.

At length he said, "It begins with a man named Leonid Cheznev. For three years he's been one of several deputy ministers at the Ministry of Energy of the Russian Federation. The ministry is responsible for drafting and implementing national policy in the oil and fuel sector, including all issues relating to electric power, gas supplies, oil production, land and sea pipelines and future energy sources.

"He became an expert in his field after graduating from the Moscow Power Engineering Institute where he majored in utilities. He had never appeared on our radar screens and we regarded him as just another nerdy official within the Russian government."

Dean paused to light a cigarette. He took his time about it, working out in his mind how best to explain things to a layman.

"That was until three months ago," he went on. "Cheznev got word to one of our operatives in Moscow that he wanted to come over to the West — in other words defect. He wanted the usual terms, money and a new identity in the States. Naturally we jumped at the chance to bring him over."

"Which means he has a pile of information that you want to get your hands on," I said.

Dean nodded. "Indeed he does. You see, Cheznev was until recently a member of a highly secret committee that was set up by the Kremlin to develop Russia's strategic policy in the Arctic over the coming decade. But he discovered that he didn't like what was being planned. He became disillusioned and tried to get things changed from within.

"But he was unsuccessful and got kicked off the committee. At about the same time he suffered a personal tragedy when his wife was killed in a car crash. After that he decided it was time to start a new life in the west. That's when he approached us."

"So what information does he have to sell?" I asked.

Dean stirred his coffee, the spoon clinking noisily against the china cup. Then he said, "As you probably know the Arctic region was the focus of a lot of aggressive posturing during the Cold War. But afterwards tensions eased and military bases were scaled back.

"But in recent years things have changed thanks to the combination of increasing energy prices and accelerating climate change. Nations, including the US and the UK, are racing to carve up Arctic resources as the ice retreats."

"That doesn't surprise me," I said. "I've seen the figures. They say that oil reserves off Greenland are as big as those in the north sea."

Dean nodded. "That's correct. A US Geological Survey estimates that twenty per cent of the world's remaining oil and natural gas supplies are located in the Arctic. And this, of course, raises all kinds of national security issues. We know, for instance, that Russia has set up a dedicated military force up here and has even staked a claim to the seabed beneath the North Pole.

"This has led to fears that we're heading for another Cold War or even a full-on confrontation between Russia and the Nato countries. The Kremlin has insisted publicly that there are no plans for any armed intervention in the future. It says it wants fruitful multilateral co-operation and collaboration.

"But we've suspected for a long time that they've been developing a secret strategy and it turns out we were right. Cheznev revealed a few nuggets of information to us to whet our appetite. It was clear to see why his conscience persuaded him to change sides. He says their planned military build-up in the Arctic is on a far bigger scale than we've been led to believe. They're also planning to construct new bases above and below the Arctic Circle. More warships and subs will patrol the region. And they aim to seize new shipping routes that open up as the ice melts."

"And Cheznev is prepared to give you all the details," I said.

Dean nodded. "He's got the lot. Strategy documents. Photos. Statistics. Once we have it we can confront the Russians and put pressure on them to back off. And if they won't we'll at least know where we stand."

"Sounds pretty scary," I said.

He held my gaze. "It is. And it's likely to get scarier if at some point the Russians decide to cut off our access to marine passages and natural resources."

I sat back and thought about it. I had known for some time that trouble had been brewing in the Arctic over the scramble for resources. Much of it was well-documented. But I hadn't known that nations were investing in military hardware and personnel to fight for the oil beneath the ice. That made the prospect of an eventual confrontation all the more likely.

"That's all very interesting," I said. "But what has this got to do with what's happened to me?"

"I was coming to that," Dean said. "You see, after we'd agreed to take Cheznev a plan was worked out to bring him over. He was attending an energy conference here in Reykjavik. Two of our agents got him out of the hotel and took him to the domestic airport in the early hours. We had a small plane there. It was going to fly to Kulusuk where Cheznev was to be put on a plane to the States."

"And I take it that was the plane that went down," I said.

Dean nodded. "Engine failure we believe. The weather was bad and we lost contact with them. An air and sea search was mounted when conditions improved but it was a day later and not a single piece of wreckage was found."

"I still don't see what you're getting at," I said. "What has this Cheznev business and the plane got to do with what I'm involved in?"

He sat back in his chair and caressed his left earlobe. Presently he said, "Maxwell Standish was one of the two

111

CIA agents on that plane. Both were field operatives based in Iceland."

It took a moment for this to sink in. An image of the dead man out at Mikkelson island flashed in my mind. A CIA agent for God's sake. It was a lot to get my head around.

"That explains part of it I suppose," I said. "But why did the professor have to die because a corpse from a lost plane was washed ashore a week later?"

"Five days to be exact."

"Five days, five weeks. So what?"

"Think about it."

"Save me the effort will you? I'm in no mood for guessing games."

Dean heaved himself to his feet and began pacing the room, hands clenched behind his back, pot-belly protruding through his jacket.

"The plane crashed five days ago, right? Which means that Standish couldn't have been killed when the plane went down if he'd been dead only a day or two when the Inuits found his body."

"So somehow he managed to survive for maybe as long as four days," I said.

"Precisely. It means also that the others, including Cheznev, might have survived and are perhaps still alive."

Dean studied my expression before going on. "We think that's why the Russians killed the professor and tried to kill you. And why they burned down the station with the body in it. They didn't want us to find out that Cheznev might still be out there somewhere. They feared that if we knew for sure that it was Standish we'd renew our efforts to find survivors. And they were right. "

"But how did they know about the body in the first place?" I said.

"I'm not sure. We learned about it as a matter of course from the Coast Guard. Maybe they learned about it from the same source."

"But even so, how did you know it was Standish?"

"We didn't. We were told only what Professor Brun reported to the police, that the body was that of a white man in his thirties. We were waiting for the police to get back to us. But you got there first with Sidorov and the woman. Like us the Russians were looking out for anything unusual occurring along that part of the coast. That's why those two were in Tasiilaq. FSB teams were covering all the settlements on the east coast of Greenland."

"One thing is puzzling me," Geisler said. "And that's how the Russians knew that Standish was one of your agents. It's my understanding that you didn't release the names of the passengers in the plane."

"That's right," Dean said. "We issued a statement saying only that they were still-to-be-identified businessmen. So we're assuming they got the names from the same person who told them we were bringing Cheznev out." He turned to me. "Probably the same stoolie who tipped them off about you coming to the embassy this morning. We've been trying to fish him out, but he's a clever bastard, whoever he is."

There was a long pause before anyone else spoke and then it was Geisler. "Do you think the others, including Cheznev, are still alive?" he asked.

"Who knows?" Dean said. "It's a slim chance, I'll admit, but the fact remains that Standish didn't die until five days after the plane went down. So where was he during that time?"

The Colonel leaned forward. "How he got so far away from where the plane ditched is a puzzle in itself," he said. "They may have managed to get into a life raft. But I can't imagine it would have stayed afloat for that long. The weather has been pretty bad in the Strait this past week."

"Where exactly did the plane go down?" I said.

"I'll show you."

Dean walked over to the map on the wall opposite George Washington. The rest of us got up and joined him. The map showed every detail of Iceland and Greenland and the Denmark Strait in between.

Dean pointed to a spot about two hundred miles north of Tasiilaq in the middle of the Strait. "This is where we believe the plane went down." He pointed lower down the map. "The body turned up here. Seventy odd miles away. That's a long way to travel in those conditions."

"What happens if they are still alive and the Russians find them first?" I asked.

"Cheznev will probably go to jail for life," he said. "Or he may even be executed. As for our two agents I wouldn't like to say."

114

Several minutes passed during which no one spoke. I finished off my tea, which by then was only lukewarm, and began to feel the first rumblings of hunger in my stomach.

"Wait a minute," Geisler cut in suddenly. "There is something we haven't considered," he said.

We all waited.

"An iceberg," he almost shouted. "What if the plane crashed onto an iceberg? It would explain why there was no wreckage and how Standish came to be so far south of where the plane went down."

Bridges shrugged off the suggestion. "It'd be a million to one chance."

Geisler shook his head. "Not necessarily. There are literally thousands of icebergs in the Denmark Strait at this time of year drifting south with the current. Many of them are huge fuckers the size of apartment blocks."

Without any warning the Colonel sprang to his feet. He declared loudly. "My God, you may be right."

"What do you mean?" Dean said.

"Two days ago the pilot of a private plane crossing the Strait reported seeing a figure on an iceberg about twenty miles out from the Greenland coast. We didn't attach any significance to it at the time, but now..."

Dean cut him short. "Why wasn't I told about this?"

The Colonel reddened. "It didn't occur to us. The pilot assumed what he saw was a polar bear. He said the light was poor so he didn't get a good look."

"Why didn't he fly back over the berg to check it out?"

"I seem to remember that he did, but he couldn't find the same berg. Apparently the area was full of 'em. He couldn't go on looking for long because his fuel reserves were low."

"Where exactly was this berg seen?" Dean asked.

The Colonel thought for a moment. "About a hundred miles north of Tasiilaq."

"Okay," Dean said. "Get the planes to concentrate on that area. I know this is all only guesswork, but at least it's better than searching more miles than we can handle without any idea what we're looking for." He turned to Geisler. "You really think this is a possibility?"

Geisler showed no sign of doubt. "Those icebergs are huge. A plane could crash onto it and quite conceivably stay there."

Dean rose to his feet. "Gentleman. I think for now we'll assume there might well be survivors and that they could be marooned somewhere in the Denmark Strait on an iceberg. We might as well concentrate all our efforts in that direction since we've got nowhere else to go."

"I suggest we co-ordinate the operation from Kalusuk in Greenland," the Colonel said. "That's close to where the berg was spotted. We've already got a plane there and we can send a helicopter down."

Dean nodded and turned to Bridges. "You go out to Kulusuk, Roy. Help organize the search. It will mean having a man on the spot. Leave right away."

Dean then looked at me. "Are you desperately anxious to get home, Mr Preston?"

116

The question caught me by surprise. "Well it would be good to freshen up and get some rest," I said. "I also need to inform the insurers about my plane and decide where to go from here."

"Well I've got a proposition for you. We'll help you with the insurance stuff if you help us."

"How'd you mean?"

"You know the Denmark Strait and the Greenland coastline as well as anyone. I'm sure you've flown over it enough times. So I think it would be a good idea if you tagged along with Roy. You can be a paid advisor."

"Are you serious?" I said.

"I'm deadly serious, Mr Preston. You're as much involved as anyone in this. I'm not asking you to take any risks. Just go back to Kalusuk and assist Roy."

I hesitated, but not for long. The thought of going back to my house, which was an empty shell at the best of times, didn't much appeal. And besides, I was keen to see how things developed.

"Very well," I said. "Count me in."

THIRTEEN

They kitted me out with some new clothes at the embassy, but I didn't have time to shower or get something to eat before Bridges sought me out and told me it was time to go.

The official embassy car took us out to the airport. The plane was waiting for us. A smart six-seat Citation Jet. I'd expected to go across to Greenland in a military aircraft but I should have known that the CIA would travel in style.

When we were snug in our seats the pilot got clearance and we were soon climbing into a sky that was clear and blue with only little strands of cotton wool cloud to mar its pristine appearance.

About four hundred miles of sea separates the stark Tasiilaq region of east Greenland from Iceland. It wasn't long before we were flying over scores of the most bizarre shaped icebergs. They had been modelled by the weather into the weirdest forms; some like giant Sphinxes, others like castles with spires and walls rising hundreds of feet into the air.

They were all heading towards the North Atlantic, but most of them would melt or crumble along the way. It was a great annual procession of broken ice from the Arctic. A weird and wonderful sight.

But as I looked down I couldn't help thinking how scary it would be if you were stranded on one of those monsters.

Totally exposed to the wild elements. The wind, the sea, the ice, the snow. And all the time knowing that sooner or later, unless you were lucky enough to be rescued, the floating island that was keeping you alive would vanish from under you.

We eventually saw the mountains of east Greenland etched razor sharp in the clear Arctic air, their summits coated in snow.

Tasiilaq wasn't far beyond. We dawdled in low over the town and descended gradually towards the offshore island of Kulusuk east of the fjord entrance. The island was soon beneath us and we came down on the small airstrip that was not much more than a flat gravel road.

I looked outside at the radar station, a dark grey incongruous mass set against a faultless sky. Nearer to the plane was the little airport building, and next to it a couple of temporary-looking huts.

As we stepped down from the plane two men wearing US air force uniforms met us.

"I'm Captain Adams," one of them said to Bridges. "I gather you're taking charge of things here."

Adams was a thin man with an aquiline face and large, staring eyes.

"That's right," Bridges said. "Anything new?"

"Not so far. We have a plane up and the Icelandic Coast Guard have a vessel in the Strait. But it's a big area – three hundred miles long and a hundred and eighty across at its narrowest."

Bridges gave a satisfied nod, then asked if accommodation had been arranged for us.

"The embassy asked me to reserve two rooms at the hotel in the village," Adams said. "But I'm afraid it's full. This is a busy time of the year. But there are three hotels over in Tasiilaq. That's a few minutes away by helicopter. So we've got you in one of those."

It was a shame because I'd stayed at the Hotel Kulusuk before and it was only a short drive from the airport. It was also a pretty comfortable place and was usually packed out during the summer months.

"Mr Preston would like to go across now," Bridges said. "I'll go after we've had a briefing."

"The helicopter shuttle is still operating," Adams said. "It'll take far less time than the ferry."

"Good." Bridges turned to me. "Get settled in then and I'll join you when I'm finished here."

"Suits me," I said.

Just then we were all distracted by the screaming engines of a Fokker 50 which was coming in to land after flying in from Iceland.

I watched its descent, marvelling at the way the pilot was able to land the giant bird on the runway. He took her to the end of it, then turned and taxied over to the airport building. I guessed it was one of the regular flights from Reykjavik.

After a while the passengers began to appear. A mixed bunch of tourists and construction workers. I figured they

120

would take the ferry over to the town. It was cheaper and able to carry far more people that the helicopter shuttle.

In fact I was the only person on the shuttle. It took just ten minutes to transport me to the little heliport in Tasiilaq. From there I walked to the hotel where a young, sallow-faced guy gave me a room overlooking the harbour. He also provided me with an overnight kit including toothbrush and razor.

The room was clean but very basic. A double bed, bathroom, writing table and TV. But it was plenty comfortable.

I undressed without hurry, then showered and shaved. The water was hot and refreshing and I let it lash my aching body for a full ten minutes, hoping it would wash away the sense of unease that had me in its grip. Afterwards I took a stroll down to the harbour, hands in pockets, drawing the fresh Greenland air into my lungs.

The boat was arriving with the visitors from Iceland. Some Inuit children had already gathered on the little landing stage as the boat drew in alongside. The boat was secured and the passengers began to alight.

I noticed a young dark-haired woman wearing a leather overcoat and carrying a suitcase. She made her way up the slope towards the hotel and I watched her with interest.

She had gone to great lengths to change her appearance, but there was no mistaking who it was. It was funny really because I never thought I'd see Gudren Bragason again.

FOURTEEN

She climbed briskly up the hill between the little wooden houses and I followed at what I judged to be a circumspect distance. I got to the hotel entrance in time to see her sign the register, pick up her case and walk upstairs.

I went in and over to the desk clerk. I told him my friend had just arrived on the ferry and described Gudren to him. He told me that Gudren Sorensdottir had just checked in. Room six.

I asked to use the phone. Bridges had given me his mobile number which I'd scrawled on the back of a piece of paper.

A minute later he answered. "Who is this?"

"Preston."

"Is everything Okay? I'll be over shortly."

"It's the woman," I said. "She's here."

"What woman?"

"Gudren Bragason, only she's using a different name and trying her damnedest to look like someone else."

"Where are you?"

"At the hotel. She arrived on that Fokker from Iceland. What shall I do?"

"Has she seen you?"

"I'm pretty sure she hasn't."

"Just stay put then. I'll come across."

"Okay, but hurry."

Half an hour later I was still sitting in the reception area looking furtively around and wondering what the hell was keeping Bridges when the desk clerk called me over. He was holding a phone to his ear. He replaced it and said, "Miss Sorensdottir would like you to go up to her room, sir."

Something happened inside me that I can't explain, but it left me feeling cold.

I said, "Are you sure she wants me?"

"That's what she said, sir."

"I'm expecting a Mr Bridges from the airfield," I said. "When he arrives send him straight up will you?"

The door to room six was slightly ajar. I pushed it open gently and stood in the doorway, ready to jump out of the way if I found myself facing some giant Russian with cropped hair. But the only person I saw was Gudren, stretched out on the bed puffing on a cigarette.

She lifted her head and said softly, "For God's sake come in if you are going to."

I stepped into the room and found she was alone.

"Leave the door open," she said. "If it makes you feel safer and more comfortable."

She moved into a sitting position on the side of the bed, outing her cigarette in an ashtray on the bedside table. Why was she so calm? I wondered. I couldn't figure it and it made me uneasy.

"It sure is a small world," she said.

"How did you know I was here?" I demanded.

"I saw you following me from the harbour. I'm afraid you'd never make a detective."

"I know what's been going on," I said. "I know you're a Russian agent."

She gave a tired grin. "I'm well aware that you've found things out courtesy of our friends in the CIA."

"So where is your psycho friend?"

"I take it you mean Viktor," she said. "Unfortunately he's been summoned back to Moscow. He's made one fuck up too many. Allowing you to get away has caused a lot of problems for us and he'll be expected to explain himself."

"And what about you? Why have you come to Greenland?"

She shrugged. "They wanted me back here to monitor developments. Now the Americans know that Cheznev might be alive there's a degree of panic among my superiors. And we have you to thank for that."

I took a step nearer and noticed that the bathroom door to my right was slightly ajar.

"I know what Sidorov did at the research station," I said. "He killed the professor and set light to the building."

She shrugged. "It became necessary after we realized that the dead man was one of the American agents who was on the aircraft with Cheznev."

"You callous bitch," I said. "The professor didn't deserve to die."

"We did what we had to do."

"It's madness," I said. "This whole thing. The world can do without another bloody Cold War."

"I totally agree, Mr Preston. But I'm afraid it's inevitable. We can't all lay claim to the same natural resources."

"So your country's answer is to get in first and keep the rest of us out."

"That's a rather stark analysis."

"But it's true," I said. "It's why you're desperate to stop Cheznev from revealing the details of your plans. You know they will stir up a shit storm."

"We want to stop Cheznev because he's a traitor," she said. "He wants to betray his country. We can't allow him to do that."

She took another cigarette from the packet on the bedside table and lit it. I was still surprised that she seemed so calm and unruffled having been exposed. But I was sure she wouldn't feel so confident when Bridges showed up. So what the devil was keeping him?

Gudren checked her watch.

"Expecting someone?" I said.

She casually blew out a plume of smoke.

"In a few minutes two men will arrive here to escort me to the survey ship in the harbour," she said. "Once on board I'll be on Russian territory and therefore out of harm's way. So there's just time to bid you a fond farewell, Mr Preston. I'm sorry for all the trouble you've been through. You'll be glad to know that now the cat's out of the bag you no longer pose a threat to us. So there's no longer any need for you to die."

I felt a sudden urge to hurl myself across the room and slap the woman. But I didn't get a chance to follow it through because just then I heard a sound behind me.

I started to turn just as something hard and heavy came crashing down on the back of my head.

The last thing I saw was the carpet coming up to meet me.

*

When I came around my head was spinning, throbbing and screaming all at once. I forced my eyelids open and saw Bridges standing over me.

"What the hell happened to you?" he said, as if it wasn't obvious.

He placed both hands under my armpits and lifted me up.

"Who did it?" he asked.

I shook my aching head and took a deep, rasping breath. "I don't know. I was talking to the woman." I looked around. "Where is she?"

"The door was open so I came straight in," Bridges said. "Found you here. There was nobody else."

I staggered over to the window. Stared out. I could see Gudren from the window. She hadn't gone far, but there was no hope of catching her. She was sitting in the prow of a small outboard powered boat with two men and the boat was chugging across the water towards the survey ship Lamanov.

126

I pointed her out to Bridges. "There's the bitch."

"Once she's on board she's as good as in the Kremlin," he said.

"Someone must have been hiding in the bathroom," I said. "Or maybe came in through the door before you did."

"Well there's nothing we can do about it now. But look, there's some makeshift accommodation over at the airport. It was put up recently for teams carrying out renovation work. I suggest we both check out of the hotel and stay over there tonight. Might be safer."

FIFTEEN

Two prefabricated buildings had been erected close to the terminal block. They contained several rooms, a recreation area and a bar. And not much more.

I was given a room of my own after a doctor examined my head and assured me that no serious damage had been done. He gave me some pain killers. Afterwards I went to the recreation hall. There were half a dozen guys in there, sitting at small plastic-topped tables chatting desultorily among themselves. Bridges was standing at the bar in his flying jacket, looking like one of those Battle of Britain pilots.

"What suits you?" he asked.

"Whisky," I said. It wasn't my favourite drink by any means but I felt I needed a kick in the gut after what I'd been through.

Bridges ordered the drinks and some sandwiches.

"Great," I said. "I'm famished."

"Me too. How's the head?"

"There's a bump about the size of a fist. But the doc says I'll live"

"You don't look too bad I'm glad to say."

My whisky arrived and I swallowed some, feeling it bite into the back of my throat. It tasted good.

"Any luck so far with the search?"

He shook his head. "Between you and me I'm not sure we aren't wasting our time."

"What do you mean?"

"Well, this theory about an iceberg; it seems a bit far-fetched to me. What do you think?"

"I'm inclined to agree with your boss. It's a slim chance, but the fact remains that the other guys who were on the plane are still missing."

"But that doesn't mean they're alive."

"It doesn't mean they're dead either."

We drank in silence for a spell. Then, changing the subject, I asked, "How long have you been in Iceland?"

He was leaning on the bar, one elbow pressed into a pool of spilled drink. "Two years," he said.

"And before that?"

"CIA headquarters in Washington."

"What made you come this far north?"

"Needed a change of scenery I guess. A vacancy arose so I applied for it."

For the next half an hour the conversation moved along spontaneously as we downed a couple more glasses of whisky and scoffed the thick, crusty ham sandwiches. It was nine in the evening and I should have been dog-tired. Instead, I was running on gallons of adrenalin.

Just after nine thirty Adams came into the bar. The look on his face was enough to tell us that something was up. He charged across the room, knocking over a chair that stood in his way. When he reached us he said between gasps, "I just heard from our pilot. He's just flown over a large

129

iceberg. He says there are people on it - along with a wrecked aircraft."

SIXTEEN

It took time for this to sink in even though it should have come to neither of us as a complete surprise.

"Where is the berg?" Bridges asked.

"Sixty miles north of here and about forty miles out from the coast. It's a big one apparently in an area of clear water. But there's a problem. Fog is closing in rapidly."

"Can we get a chopper up there?"

"Ours isn't here yet," Adams said. "And the shuttle wouldn't be any good because it's too small."

"What about the Coast Guard?"

"They're sending a ship to the area but it's about four hours away. A search and rescue helicopter is on standby for when the fog clears."

"But this is crazy," Bridges said. "Are you actually saying that we can't get to them?"

Adams shrugged. "Not right away, sir."

Bridges shook his head. "Shit. We can't just hang around. We might lose them again or the berg might collapse."

"I'll get back to the Coast Guard and see what can be done," Adams said.

Bridges turned to me.

"You know what goes on out there. How long is this fog likely to last?"

"Could be less than an hour," I said. "Or it could be days. Quick forming fog is a major hazard in the Strait. The Coast Guard know what to expect which is why they're holding back. But from what I'm hearing it may not have closed in on the berg yet. So there's always the possibility that conditions will change suddenly."

Bridges arched his brow. "Then what would you do?"

I shrugged. "I'd probably take a chance and go for it. You can always turn back if the weather closes in."

"It's a pity you haven't got your plane. Can you fly a chopper?"

"I'm afraid not."

"Damn."

And then a thought struck him. "I saw a seaplane over in the town," he said.

I nodded. "The Otter. It belongs to Bill Osborn. He's a friend."

Adams started to say something but Bridges shut him up and said to me, "Could we take that?"

"I'm not sure," I told him. "We'd have to ask him."

"And if he says we can will you take me up?"

I thought about those men clinging to life on the iceberg and said, "Sure. Why not?"

Adams was aghast. "But this is insane."

Bridges turned on him. "We have no choice. It's imperative that we get to the berg as quickly as possible. I can't tell you why exactly but I can say that it's a matter of national security."

Adams hesitated. "But the Coast Guard are saying it isn't safe."

"Fuck the Coast Guard," Bridges said. "They have no idea what's at stake here."

Fifteen minutes later Bridges and I were in town looking for Bill Osborn. We eventually found him in a small locals bar near the waterfront. He was slouched over a corner table surrounded by bottles, and if someone had struck a match he probably would have gone up in flames.

It took perhaps five minutes to get some sense from him. Through a spluttering of curses he confirmed that the Otter was in working order and said the keys were in his breast pocket. I don't think he quite realized that we intended using it as he watched through bleary eyes as we hurried out of the bar.

*

The controls of all small aircraft are more or less the same and it didn't take me long to familiarize myself with the cockpit of the Otter. Having made sure there was an inflatable life raft and some flares on board we were off. As we headed out of the harbour I noticed that the Lamanov was upping anchor, which seemed an odd coincidence. I also saw that there was a helicopter on the helipad which hadn't been there yesterday morning when I arrived.

The water was calm and take-off was without incident. We climbed to six hundred feet and I set her on course for the co-ordinates Adams had given me before we left the airfield.

I got weather reports over the radio and the threat of fog had not receded. The Coast Guard tried to persuade us to turn back, saying that what we were doing was reckless. But Bridges told me to ignore them and plough on.

Under normal circumstances I would have played safe and turned around. Seaplanes are not great in foul weather. But these were not normal circumstances. At least two men were stranded on an iceberg that could topple over at any time. If there was even the slightest chance of rescuing them then I was determined to go for it.

And then there was the bigger picture to consider. The information that the Russian defector was willing to impart to the Americans. I felt I had a personal stake in ensuring that he managed to achieve his goal.

We eventually saw the fog bank ahead of us. It was rolling southwards at an alarming rate.

Five minutes later, after circling the area, we spotted the iceberg.

It was in a large area of open water. The nearest other berg was about a quarter of a mile away.

It was shaped somewhat like a badly constructed church. The main chunk of ice reared up to well over a hundred feet above the water and was roughly a thousand feet long and five hundred feet wide. At one end was a tower of solid ice. It rose vertically like a frozen finger and reaching a further eighty or so feet into the sky.

The base of this tower was about sixty feet in diameter and it narrowed as it grew, looking particularly unsafe all the way to the top. Crouched against the base of the tower was the Beechcraft. The tail unit, which seemed intact, was pointing up at an angle and the long distinctive nose of the plane was buried inside the ice.

The fuselage did not appear to be severely damaged and there was no sign that a fire had broken out. A deep trench in the ice snaked drunkenly away from the wreckage, presumably gouged by the plane as it slithered on its belly across the berg before crashing into the tower.

They were indeed lucky. If the tower hadn't been there they would have gone right off the other side of the berg. The trench started on the very edge of the berg's highest cliff, which probably meant that the part on which it had actually landed had broken off.

The sides of the iceberg were sheer for the most part, cliffs plunging into black frothy water. There was only one exception to the uniformity of the sides, in an area where the cliff had fallen away to form a near flat slope that started at the top of the berg and ended in a short drop just above the water.

As I looked down I saw a dark speck on the ice near the wreckage. I took us down for a closer look and saw that the speck was actually a man and he was waving his arms about frantically.

I turned to Bridges. "The fog's moving in fast. I reckon it will envelop the berg in ten to fifteen minutes."

135

"Does that give us time to get down there and up again?"

"Not really. Getting them off the berg will be tricky."

"So what if you take me down and drop me off?" Bridges said. "I'll use the raft to get onto the berg and you can get airborne again."

"So you want me to leave you?"

"That's right. I've got the survival kit. I can help out until we can rescue them."

"Are you sure about that? It's a big risk."

"Let me worry about that," he said. "You just make sure you get back out of here before that fog arrives."

Three minutes later we hit the water and I taxied towards the sloping side of the berg. There was a slight breeze from the north and the surface had a scaly appearance, but it wasn't rough.

From the air the berg had seemed big enough, but now that we were looking up instead of down it was brought into a new, terrifying perspective. It was a great white monster that could have screened a five-storey building. At its base the berg was coloured greeny-blue with clefts of deep purple and higher up it was brilliant white, sparkling like an expensive diamond.

I brought the Otter to a halt about fifty yards from the berg, swallowed by its great shadow.

"I'll go on from here in the raft," Bridges said.

He tossed the raft out of the cabin door and it inflated automatically. Then he strapped the survival kit to his back and climbed out.

"Well done, Preston," he said. "We owe you."

I glanced up at the berg and saw that the man who had been waving to us was now stationed at the top of the slope. He wasn't much bigger even now, nothing more than a stain against the prevailing whiteness behind him.

Bridges climbed into the raft and shoved away from the floats, moving deeper into the shadow of the berg.

But he had gone only about fifty feet when something else seized my attention and set my heart racing.

It was a helicopter.

SEVENTEEN

The chopper appeared suddenly from the other side of the berg and hovered above it like an angry red bird seeking out its prey. Then it descended in a sudden rush towards the lowest side of the berg, the downwash of air from its powerful rotors churning the ice into a wall of white cloud.

Almost at once I recognized it as the helicopter from the Lamanov. I watched as its narrow tail swung round and then in the opening in its side, I saw a man crouched low aiming a rifle at the raft. A shot exploded and the bullet punctured the water near to the raft.

Bridges didn't try to turn around. He sank the paddles deeper into the water and the little craft jogged on towards the berg.

Another shot rang out. This time the raft wavered slightly and Bridges leaned awkwardly to one side. There was no time to follow their progress any further. I had to get out of there. I swung the Otter round and pushed on the power. But I didn't get far. The helicopter came down in front of me like a bomb, stopping just above the water as if suspended on string.

I pulled the Otter to the left to avoid a collision, slowed and heard the power ooze from the engine with a deafening shriek. The helicopter next appeared above me to starboard and this time the man inside was lining up his sights.

I ducked and heard a thud as the bullet crashed into the door. Another shot and the bullet slammed into the roof. I risked a quick look, saw that the berg was dead ahead and approaching fast.

The Otter had turned in an arc and if I didn't do something quick she'd slam right into it. So I jerked her to port. Another bullet smashed through the windscreen and tore a hole in the co-pilot's seat.

The groan of the rotor blades altered position above me. I sat up and through the shattered windscreen I could see the jagged white cliff on my right.

The helicopter dropped from the sky again about fifteen yards ahead. Instinctively I veered away from it, but in my panic I chose the wrong direction.

The port wing ploughed into the side of the berg with a loud crunching sound. The Otter spun uncontrollably and the propeller blades drilled into the ice wall. I prayed she'd stop before blowing up. An avalanche of ice was showering the tiny plane, raining big white boulders that shook her from side to side.

When finally she came to a stop my heart wasn't where it should have been. I sat up and looked out. The Otter was snuffling the lowest side of the berg, port wing in shreds and wedged into the ice.

I realized then that the helicopter had lost interest in me and was now hovering above a head that showed just above the water. Bridges was swimming for it towards the berg. The raft was floating aimlessly nearby, shrinking into a black shapeless blob. Bridges had about twenty yards to go to the lee of the berg.

The Russian's rifle barked again. The bullet hissed into the water inches from his head.

Bridges swam on a few yards then submerged. The helicopter moved in for the kill. But no more shots were fired, for suddenly the helicopter began gaining height, sheering up over the berg. The reason for its sudden departure became startlingly obvious as I looked through the window.

The wall of fog had arrived and was about to swallow us up.

EIGHTTEEN

The helicopter vanished behind the berg's high tower and the throb of its engine grew fainter. On this side of the berg the water became relatively calm again, mirroring the blanket of grey that was moving in.

In the hope that it might still be working I tried the radio. Not surprisingly there was no response. I pushed open the side door and looked blearily about me. I had been lucky in one respect. The Otter had halted against the lowest side of the berg where the wall of ice rose about nine feet out of the water.

I ducked back into the cabin and rummaged among the junk on the floor. I collected flares, first-aid kit, binoculars and a rope. I found a packet of cigarettes and some matches and in the map compartment was Bill Osborn's revolver. I checked to see if it was loaded. It was.

Then I found a blanket, laid it out and dumped all the stuff on it. Using some string from under one of the seats I tied the ends of the blanket together. Then I pushed this improvised sack out the door onto the float and crawled out after it, feeling the cold Arctic air creep into my clothes like some living thing.

I swung the sack up onto the berg and then jumped up myself, managing first time to get a purchase on the ledge and pull my elbows over the top. Soon I was sitting on the ledge trying to retrieve my breath in short, sharp gasps.

141

The ice was quite different in character to the stuff you skate on. It was wet, rough and hummocky. I would have welcomed a pair of climbing boots in place of the rubber-soled shoes I was wearing.

It was about ninety feet uphill to the wreckage. I got up, grabbed the sack and threw it over one shoulder. I trod carefully, watching all the time for hidden cracks and soft patches of ice. It was difficult to maintain a footing as the berg moved gently beneath me, swaying in the current like an unsteady ship.

"Preston."

I stopped, held my breath. The voice had come from behind, but there was nothing but the ice that rolled unevenly into the fog.

"Over here."

His head surfaced a few yards back above the edge of the slope.

"Bridges!" I gasped.

I dropped the sack and moved quickly to him. "Are you all right?"

He was shivering. "Just about. I managed to climb up here, but now I'm stuck."

I knelt and looked over. He was standing on a narrow ledge that rose up from the water.

"I'd given you up for drowned," I said.

"I went under. When I surfaced the 'copter had gone."

"The fog," I pointed out unnecessarily.

"Well come on then," he said gruffly. "Help me the hell up from here."

I pointed to the sack. "There's a blanket over there. Do you want me to get it for you?"

"No. Let's get up to the wreckage first and let them know they have company. If this fog gets any thicker we might find ourselves walking over the side."

I picked up the sack and we got under way. The slope seemed endless. The higher we climbed the steeper it seemed to get and the more laboured became our efforts. I began to wonder if the berg was not really the top of a mountain rooted beneath the sea.

By the time we reached the wreckage the fog had enfolded us and visibility was down to a matter of yards. To the right the deep trench in the ice I'd seen from the air ran into the fog.

The aircraft itself wasn't in such bad shape considering what had happened. Most of the fuselage remained intact. Though torn and fractured, both wings were still attached to it.

The blue and white paintwork was covered by a thin sheet of ice which also covered the windows. The nose and the cockpit were buried inside the ice tower.

The side door just behind the wing jerked open suddenly and a man wearing a hooded parka stepped onto the ice. At first I put him in his early thirties, but really it was hard to tell. His face was the colour of an old parchment and he had cadaverously sunken cheeks. His beard was like an unkempt bush.

"Hello Roy," he said. "I really didn't expect you to drop in."

143

"It's good to see you, man," Bridges said. "Thank God you're alive."

Bridges gestured towards me. "This is John Preston. The pilot. John, meet Paul Hudson. He's one of my colleagues in the Agency."

Hudson took a few paces forward. "What happened out there? Who were they?"

"Russians," Bridges told him. "They're still determined to stop Cheznev from coming over to us. Is he alive?"

Hudson rubbed his knuckles into his eyes and ran his tongue over mauve lips. "He's inside."

"How is he?"

"A broken arm and badly in need of medical attention, but alive."

"What about Ellroy, the pilot?"

"Dead, along with Standish."

"And how are you?"

"All right, I guess. A few cuts and bruises, plus frozen innards. But nothing I can't put up with."

I noticed that Bridges was shivering more violently and I suggested we went into the aircraft.

The cabin would have made a sufferer of claustrophobia take his chances outside. It was a six-seat layout behind the cockpit but the four passenger seats had been removed to make space. Up front in the cockpit the walls were almost touching across the crumpled seats where the pressure of the ice had forced them inwards, and the control panel was a meaningless mass of twisted metal.

Cheznev was on the floor with his legs curled up under a blanket and his left arm in a sling. He made an effort to raise his head and I saw that he was a thin, withered man in his fifties. His face was a sickly white and trenched with a thousand wrinkles. His hair was dark and thin, starting at a point in the middle of his head and receding backwards in an unruly fashion.

As we crowded into the cabin Cheznev stirred and gave a feeble little moan as he raised himself onto his good elbow. In a rich Russian accent, he said, "Are we to be rescued?"

"That was the general idea," Bridges told him ruefully, "before your former buddies showed up. Now we're stuck on this damn ice cube with you."

"The helicopter," he said listlessly. "It was Russian?"

Bridges nodded.

"Then they are after me?" There was genuine astonishment in his voice.

"I'm afraid so. But don't worry. The good guys know where we are. We'll soon be out of here."

Cheznev was showing all the signs of exposure; slurred speech, fits of shivering and a dizzy expression. He said, "Who are you?"

Bridges said simply, "American government." Then he turned to Hudson and asked, "What have you done about his arm?"

"I couldn't find anything to use as splints so I put it in the sling and shot him with some morphine I found in the first-aid kit."

145

I got one of the blankets from the makeshift sack and handed it to Bridges. "Here, get out of those wet clothes and use this to dry yourself."

Bridges did as I suggested and Hudson produced a set of clothes that he said had belonged to Ellroy.

"Put them on, Roy," he said. "They're dry."

I could hear the rush of the sea and the moan of the iceberg as it moved and twisted in the current. It wasn't very comforting to know that we were on something with about as secure a future as a lump of sugar in a cup of scalding tea.

"What happened to the others?" Bridges said.

Hudson pushed back the hood of his parka to reveal long wavy hair. "As you can see from the state of the cockpit Ellroy didn't stand a chance."

"Where's his body?"

"We put it over the side after removing his clothes," Hudson said.

"And Standish?"

"Standish went three days ago. We were closer to land then, could even see the mountains. He was standing on a part of the berg that broke off in rough weather. There was nothing I could do to save him."

"His body was found close to the shore," Bridges said. "That's when we and the Russians realized that the rest of you might still be alive."

Bridges went on to explain how the Russians had got on to it. I don't think Cheznev was listening because he had pulled the blankets over his head and all we could hear from that corner was his light, irregular breathing.

I took out the cigarettes I'd found on the Otter and handed them to Hudson. He accepted them with alacrity and lit one up.

"What's it been like?" I asked.

"No picnic, that's for sure."

"I can't get over the fact that you have actually managed to survive on this thing for five days."

"Without this little nest we'd have frozen to death the first day," he said.

"What about food?"

"We made do for the first couple of days on what we had with us. Since that's been gone we haven't eaten."

"What's it been like?" Bridges asked.

"Terrifying. Bits of the berg have broken off every day. The part that took Standish was the size of a house." He paused, then added, "I don't think it'll be long before the tower goes. I've heard some strange noises. It could be cracking."

"That's because we're drifting into the warmer waters of the Atlantic," I said.

Hudson nodded. "I figured that.

"So what happened when you left Reykjavik?" Bridges asked.

Hudson drew deeply on his cigarette. "We headed for Kulusuk as planned, but we flew into a blizzard. Then the engine suddenly failed on us. Ellroy put out distress signals, but we didn't know if they were being picked up because we couldn't get any reception. Then we lost altitude. Ellroy yelled for us to brace ourselves and the next thing I knew we crashed into the berg. I'm not sure if it was Ellroy's intention or just luck. I was knocked unconscious and when I came round Standish told me that Ellroy was dead."

"How long were you in the blizzard?" Bridges asked.

"The entire night. It was awful. We shot up some flares but no one saw them."

"We have more flares," Bridges said. "And the Coast Guard must have a fix on us. So let's hope we're picked up before this bastard melts under us."

NINETEEN

The hours passed and they seemed like days. The monster beneath us made a racket not dissimilar to a set of giant teeth grinding incessantly into a megaphone. At one time I got up to see what it was like outside, but my vision took me only a few yards into the fog.

There was no point discussing ways of getting off the iceberg because there were none. We were trapped. Hudson had already resigned himself to this and Bridges and I were learning to fast.

Late into the night Cheznev began to moan loudly.

"Exposure," Hudson commented drowsily. "It's much worse."

"Isn't there anything we can do?" I said.

"Let's put him between us," Bridges said.

So that was what we did. We got him on his side and I snuggled up behind him in the spoon position. Bridges lay in front of him.

I pressed myself up against the old man and Bridges did the same. Hudson threw more blankets on top for extra insulation, then climbed in behind me.

And before long we were all asleep. It was a brief respite from the perilous situation we were in.

*

I was falling from a cliff into a sea that was being whipped into a frenzy by a fierce, screaming wind. High black swells were throwing themselves against the rocks at the bottom and bursting into flames of bright, white foam. Although I couldn't stop myself it seemed as if I were falling in slow motion. But I didn't hit the water. Bridges woke me just in time.

"The fog's cleared," he was saying. "Come and look outside."

I sat up, let the blankets fall away, and rubbed the sleep from my eyes.

Bridges turned and with his head lowered he went to the door. Reluctantly, I dragged myself to my feet and climbed over Hudson and Cheznev who were both still asleep.

"Brace yourself."

Bridges opened the door and stepped outside. I followed.

Without knowing what to expect I wasn't prepared for what greeted me. The fog had cleared and the wind, an eerie, shrieking force was blowing with an intensity I had seldom heard. It was scouring up millions of minute ice crystals from the surface of the berg and was carrying them within itself to form low ghostly clouds that jumped crazily about the ice.

The cabin door got pinned back against the fuselage. I stood in front of it to shield it from the wind and pulled it shut.

I heard Bridges calling, but before turning I looked up at that threatening tower of ice that loomed above the wreckage like some sinister figure in a white cloak. What would happen if it suddenly collapsed just didn't bear thinking about. I tore my eyes away from it and clambered awkwardly over the ice to Bridges. He was standing near the edge of the berg's highest precipice, pointing out to sea, his eyes squinting as defence against the wind.

The Denmark Strait was littered with icebergs for as far as the eye could see. Wild foaming water lay between them. The swells were rising to about ten feet and the indiscriminate wind raked off their caps in great white blasts. Overhead the sky was a low grey ceiling of hurrying clouds and some of the bergs were so huge their summits seemed almost to be touching it.

Some were flat-topped tabular bergs from the polar ice-cap itself, but most were of glacier origin, great freshwater monuments seemingly carved out of chalk by an abstract artist with an obsession for originality.

There was a tremendous roar as part of an iceberg, about half a mile away, broke off and plunged into the sea with a terrific splash. The explosion echoed among the other bergs as it thundered across the water.

I followed Bridges back past the wreckage to the other side of the berg. Here the cliff plunged into the water eighty or ninety feet below us. It occurred to me that if most of the berg's bulk lay beneath the water then the glacier from which had been calved must have been colossal.

On the other hand, if it was from a glacier further up the coast in north east Greenland then the berg must have been many times larger at birth. It was a frightening thought that the berg's journey to the North Atlantic was only half complete even now and before reaching its destination it would be even smaller.

"How far do you think we've drifted?" I asked, shouting to make myself heard above the wind.

"Hard to tell." He glanced at his watch. "We've been on this thing about eight hours. We could have drifted five or six miles in that time, maybe more."

I realized suddenly that my hands were turning numb with the cold. So I spat into the palms, rubbed them together and buried them in my coat pockets. In the right hand pocket I felt the revolver I'd taken from the Otter.

"Any idea how long ago the fog cleared?"

He shook his head. "I only woke up myself a few minutes before I woke you. This is how it was when I came outside. Some sight eh?"

"Do you think they've resumed the search?" I said.

"I hope so. But it doesn't mean we'll be spotted quickly. There are a lot of fucking icebergs out there."

"But what happens if the Russians find us first?"

"We just have to hope that they don't."

"What will they do with us?"

"Hopefully send us back home to avoid a major diplomatic incident."

"And what about Cheznev?"

He shrugged. "I'd rather not think about that."

Before I could ask any more questions he was heading back to the wreckage. I looked around once again, straining against the wind to see something that even remotely resembled a ship or plane. But there was nothing. Nothing that is but the endless water, the icebergs and those grey, scudding clouds.

Back in the cabin, I said, "We'll have to take turns outside. If a plane comes anywhere near we'll need to send up a flare."

"That's a point," Bridges said. "Let's say fifteen minutes each."

"I'll take the first watch, then," I said.

I fished out the revolver. "I found this on the Otter. You might as well take it."

I handed it to him.

"Thanks," he said. "I lost mine in the water."

After a while outside I got to thinking that my suggestion to have look-outs wasn't such a good one after all. I could barely manage to stand as the berg swayed and pitched in rhythm with the sea.

My face was soon numbed by the piercing, icy wind and I had to clamp my jaw tight to stop my teeth chattering. Every so often I looked up at the pinnacle of ice above the plane and kept imagining that it was departing from the vertical, bending almost imperceptibly. Nothing short of a miracle had so far prevented it from coming down on top of us.

At last my turn was up and Bridges came to relieve me. I was surprised to see Cheznev sitting up inside the cabin. His eyes were no longer vacant things in his crinkled face and he seemed fully aware of what was going on around him. He glanced up at me.

"I would like to thank you," he said.

"What for?"

"What you have done for me. For us. I am grateful."

"Don't mention it."

"Tell me, are you also with the American government?" he asked.

"Not likely," I said. "I just stumbled into this mess."

"I don't understand."

I recalled Cheznev had been sleeping when Bridges told Hudson what had been going on. So I filled him in.

"I am sorry," he said. "My actions have caused a great deal of damage."

"You can't blame yourself," I said. "You weren't to know what was going to happen."

Suddenly the little plane shuddered violently, throwing me across the floor.

It was followed by the high pitched growl of breaking ice and then an almighty splash as something large plunged into the water from a great height.

TWENTY

When the cabin was still again I found myself sprawled out on the floor. Cheznev and Hudson were next to me, total bewilderment showing on their faces.

Hudson echoed my thoughts. "The berg must be breaking up," he wailed.

The door opened and a gust of wind swept a cloud of ice dust into the cabin. Bridges came in with it and without closing the door he stood, knees bent, looking down at us. His face held a fearful expression and even before he spoke I think I knew what he was going to say.

"It's the tower," he said. "I think it's going."

I felt the surge of panic within me. "What happened out there?"

"A piece broke off on the seaward side of the tower. I didn't see it from where I was standing, but it caused the nose of the plane to jump up inside the tower and the tail to drop."

I realized then that the cabin floor was not at an angle any more.

"The ice on top of the nose must have weakened," I said.

"More likely come away altogether at the back," Bridges said.

Cheznev sat up with a jolt. "What are we going to do?" he asked.

Further thought on the subject was prevented when the cabin rolled to one side again, throwing Bridges across the floor. He rammed into Hudson and finished up across his lap. More ice was breaking outside, shaking the floor and sending out a deafening roar as if the very bowels of the earth were being mangled by some giant hand.

It lasted for about thirty seconds, then the cabin was still again, lying at an angle on the ice.

We listened to the soughing of that cold Arctic wind that was driving its heavy fist against the skin of the fuselage. There was also the sound of the sea, a pulsating, demonical cry that rose and fell like the waves, reminding us that the weather's store of spleen is exhaustible.

"We'll have to move out of here," Bridges said.

"What then?" Cheznev asked, his voice near to panic. "Where can we go? Anywhere on the iceberg will be just as unsafe."

He was right, of course. Whatever was going to happen we could not run away from it.

Bridges spoke almost in a whisper, as if he were trying hard to contain himself. "I propose we move everything to the other side of the berg. At least the tower won't fall right on top of us."

"But supposing it doesn't come down?" I said.

"Hell, we all heard it didn't we?"

"We heard ice falling," I said, "but that doesn't mean the whole thing is coming down. If we camp out there and it doesn't collapse we'll freeze to death in no time."

"But it could fall the other way," Bridges said. "So it might not damage the rest of the berg." He got to his feet and headed for the door. "It's no good talking about it. Let's go see what's happened. The berg seems still enough now."

Hudson and I followed and Cheznev stayed put.

From where the three of us stood on the ice the only apparent alteration in the whole scene was the position of the aircraft. She now lay more drunkenly than ever. Her nose was still buried in the ice, but now there was a crack above her some six feet long by six inches wide. I assumed this had opened up when the nose had reared up inside the ice.

I turned to Hudson. "Is there any way we can get around to the seaward side of the tower?"

"You crazy?" blurted Bridges.

I ignored him and looked to where Hudson was pointing.

"Over there is a ledge," he said. "It goes around the back. Standish went along it once and said it was safe enough provided you were careful."

"I still think we should move everything out of the Beech before it's too late," Bridges said. "At least over there we'll have a chance even if the tower falls inwards."

I said, "But our point is that it might not be coming down and if it isn't we'd be sitting out here freezing our balls off for God knows how long."

"Then what have you in mind, Preston?"

"One of us will have to see what damage there is. If the tower does look like it's about to fall then by all means we vacate the Beech."

"You can count me out of any heroics," Hudson said.

Bridges looked at me. "This is your idea." Which was true. I was committed.

"How wide is the ledge?"

"Come see for yourself."

Hudson led us across the ice to where the ledge started. It turned out to be about four feet wide. We couldn't see much further than fifteen feet along it as it curved with the tower. I stepped forward carefully and glanced over. It was a straight plunge to where the sea was being whipped into a detergent froth against the bottom of the cliff.

"Have you a lifejacket?"

Hudson nodded. "In the plane. I'll get it."

He went and got a bright orange lifejacket and attached it to me. "Good luck."

I took that first nerve-racking step onto the ledge and was actually surprised when it didn't collapse under me. Each step after that required a conscious effort of will-power. I trod carefully, making sure my footing was secure before placing my weight on it.

My back was pressed firmly against the cold, wet wall and my eyes were glued on the area just ahead. After several seconds I couldn't feel the wind anymore and after a few more steps I couldn't see Bridges or Hudson when I looked back.

I was alone, but being watched by hundreds of drifting icebergs. They moved in a mass of white, like some strange family of sea animals in flight from the frozen north. One berg, a monster as big as the one we were on, was only about a hundred yards away.

I moved on prudently, the ice slippery under my shoes. The ledge followed the tower, but it didn't go all the way round. It ended where there was a huge cavernous gash in the ice wall.

It went deep inside the tower, probably to where the nose of the aircraft had penetrated. I realized that the tower was about as safe as a construction of playing cards in a draughty room.

I stood for a long time without moving, trying to build up the courage to start back, wary now that the slightest sound or sudden movement could bring it all down on top of me.

True to form I chose the wrong moment to move off. The berg swayed in the current, the ledge went with it, and I lost my footing. I tried clawing at the ice, but there was nothing to hold. My legs vanished from under me and my backside dropped painfully onto the ledge. My right leg went over first and the left followed. I tried to counteract the movement by leaning into the wall and digging my fingers into the ledge. But it was no use. I couldn't stop myself. The sea bounded up at me, filling my vision for one terrifying moment; a vast abysmal grave with plenty of room for yet another wretched soul.

Somehow, though, I managed to roll over with the fall. It meant I was on my belly, still dropping, but in a position now to grab for the ledge. The sharp serrated angle of ice sawed at my armpits; then the elbows, tearing at both sleeves.

Finally the hands made contact with the edge of the precipice and held on. Miraculously. I was hanging like a dead leaf from the thinnest part of a tree in an autumn gale. Below me the sea roared, the wind slewed across the face of the cliff as the berg altered position slightly.

My arms felt as if they were being torn from the sockets, but by the grace of God my fingers clung firmly to the ledge.

Then I started pulling, straining every muscle in my arms to breaking point. Eventually I managed to get my elbows onto the ledge. Then I pulled myself up.

After getting my breath back I climbed to my feet and pigeon-stepped it back along the ledge. Bridges and Hudson were standing where I'd left them, anxious to learn the worst.

I spared them the details. "We'll have to move," I said.

"Is it bad?" Bridges asked.

"Half of it is missing back there. But you were right. At least over the other side of the berg we might stand half a chance — if luck is on our side."

The three of us trampled back to the wreckage. I told them in more detail what I had found. Afterwards Bridges and I went across to the other side of the berg in search of a suitable site. We decided to set up camp between a couple of hummocks in the hope that it would provide some protection against the wind. We got to work removing all the gear from the Beech and taking it across. It didn't take long and soon we were looking back at the crippled aircraft from the opposite side of the berg.

Cheznev sank to the ice in what appeared to be a kind of stupor, lay on his back and covered himself with blankets. The rest of us were about to do the same when Hudson gave a cry of alarm.

I spun round and followed his stricken gaze. Because the berg had twisted in the current we could see that other berg — the one I'd noticed closing in from the ledge. Now it was only about ten yards away and it was startlingly obvious that the two giant islands of ice were going to collide.

TWENTY ONE

We watched, horrified, as the towering cliffs of the two bergs came together. In the channel between them the water was white with swirling foam.

The point of impact was going to be just to the right of the ice tower and I'm sure there was no doubt in any of our minds that the tower would not stand up to it. None of us moved or made any attempt to cry out. We stood like statues, awed by the thought of what was to come. There was nowhere to run and nowhere to hide.

When the crash came it was like the end of the world. There was one hell of an explosion as the two mountains of ice bore into one another. The impact must have been many times greater than two fast-moving express trains crashing head on inside a tunnel.

The ice quivered beneath us and the distant horizon swept up at an angle as I was thrown onto my face. Then I was tossed around on the hard bumpy surface; rolling and twisting as the berg convulsed in a frightening spasm. The air was filled with a thunderous drumming noise, deafening in its intensity.

Ice crumbled all around us. Great boulders plunged into the sea throwing up leviathan spouts of spray that showered the top of the berg like rain.

I tried to get to my feet. The berg jolted, throwing me on my face again. Blindly I slid across the ice and careered into a hummock. Again the floor shuddered, reared up and fell, and this time I found myself sliding the other way, scooping up mouthfuls of loose powdery ice as my face shovelled into the surface of the berg.

An agonizing scream from close by was muffled by the ear-splitting crackle of breaking ice. I fought desperately to steady myself and just managed to see Bridges and Hudson trying to disentangle themselves from one another.

The whole scene was a nightmare of confusion, noise and sheer terror. And it seemed to go on and on.

Actually, it could only have lasted a couple of minutes, but by the time it was over I had more dents and bruises than a prize fighter.

The berg was still, though. I was lying on my belly, right cheek numb against the ice. Weakly I pushed myself to my knees, paused for a moment to gain equilibrium, then got to my feet.

Bridges and Hudson were sitting side by side behind me. Cheznev was crawling on his good arm out from under the blanket. I looked to where the two bergs had come together. The other berg had driven a good twenty feet into the berg we were on and where they were merged there was a high ridge of sharp broken ice.

Then it happened, as was inevitable.

At first it seemed to occur in slow motion, collapsing in on itself like a carefully detonated chimney. Huge rocks of ice crashed down and dented the surface of the berg in front of me. Then the bulk of the tower crumbled all at once and I went flying on my face again.

There was a sound like thunder; the berg shook; the low grey sky spun wildly above me. Once again I collided with that hummock and for the second time it saved me from sliding across the berg.

But Hudson wasn't so lucky. Out of the corner of my eye I saw him hurtle into the hummock not five yards away. Whereas I had rebounded off it he somersaulted sharply and went over the top. He cried out, tried to grab the top of the hummock, but couldn't. His death cry was lost in the thunder of the disaster as he plunged over the side of the berg into the icy sea.

About twenty seconds later the floor fell back to the horizontal and the berg became reasonably steady. I scrambled to my feet and glanced over the hummock. Where once the tower had stood millions of tons of ice formed a huge mountain. There was no sign of the aircraft. It had been completely covered.

It took a moment for it to click that the mountain of ice was moving away. I stepped onto the hummock and saw why. The berg had broken in two just beyond the hummock. It had snapped completely and the jagged cliffs were drifting apart. The half with the disintegrated tower was still merged with the other berg and as this complete white mass drew away I could see that the water was boiling furiously between the cliffs. I noticed that Bridges was watching the scene with a look of horror on his face. Cheznev, poor soul, was still wrestling with the blanket.

Bridges staggered over to me, shouting, "Where's Hudson?"

164

I pointed at the water. We could see his face-down body being buffeted by the waves.

"He's dead," I said. "I saw him go over the side."

Bridges stood there for a moment staring down into the sea, disbelief evident in his eyes. We both knew there was nothing we could do. And we knew also that it was probably only a matter of time before we met the same fate.

We both flopped onto the ice next to the Russian. There was only one thing to do and that was to try to keep warm. It had been bad enough inside the cabin, but this was ten times worse. Without the walls of the plane to stop the wind it was much, much colder and none of us was adequately dressed for such conditions. After a while I was shaking uncontrollably.

Bridges and I were on either side of Cheznev and we had to hold tight to the blankets as the wind tried to carry them away. Needless to say, I didn't sleep. I just lay there listening to the wind and the sea and praying that it wouldn't go on much longer.

My mind kept flashing back to Hudson going over the side. If I lived through this I knew the image would haunt me for the rest of my life. But at least he had been spared this agonizing prelude to what might be a slow and more painful death.

I think about two more hours passed as we lay huddled under the blankets like that. Like three lost children.

Then, suddenly, I saw the ship.

TWENTY TWO

Somehow we had managed to survive. It's open to doubt whether we'd have done so had there not come about a sudden change in the weather.

One moment the tormented cry of the wind was loud above us and the next there was only the sound of the waves lunging against the side of the berg.

I found it difficult to move at first because I'd been all but frozen solid in a screwed up position on my side. Slowly I got to my feet and flexed my muscles.

The scene around us was much the same, dark blue sea covered with icebergs, but the sky was now an uncompromising cobalt blue, streaked with small cotton wool clouds. I looked all around, but there was no sign of land in any direction.

And that was when I saw the ship.

At first I thought it was just another iceberg, but I looked twice because I couldn't be absolutely sure.

I found the binoculars and put my eyes to them. The dark shape came into focus and there was no mistaking what it was. I roused the others and started groping for the flares.

"What is it?" Bridges said.

"A ship."

I have yet to see a man move as fast as Bridges did on hearing that. In half a second he had turned over and sprung to his feet, where he stood looking around.

"Where for God's sake?"

I threw him the binoculars and pointed. "You'll need these. It seems to be heading from right to left."

"It's a ship all right," Bridges said, "but is it ours?"

"Does it matter?"

"I guess not."

I found the flares and ripped one from its waterproof container. I aimed it at the sky and fired. The gadget made a cracking sound and the chemical bomb rocketed upwards. At a reasonable height it exploded, emitting a spray of red smoke. Bridges peered again through the binoculars.

"They don't appear to have changed course," he said.

So I fired another flare.

"That's it," he yelled. "I think they've turned."

"Show me."

I handed him the flares, took the binoculars and focused on the ship.

"Thank God she's coming this way," I said. "Go on. Fire another flare."

The flare went up, making a beautiful red stain on the lush blue sky.

"Is she American?" Cheznev cried out.

I looked again, but the ship was still too far away to tell. I shrugged. "Whatever she is it won't be long before she's here."

Cheznev grinned, not very convincingly. "She must be American," he said.

But she wasn't. And she wasn't Danish or Norwegian either. She had come much closer, and I was still studying her through the binoculars when it occurred to me that the ship's lines were distinctly familiar.

I swallowed a lump the size of a football and turned to the others. "I think it's the Lamanov," I said. "The bastard must have been on our tail through the fog."

"Are you sure?" Bridges said.

"Take a look yourself."

He snatched the binoculars and looked. "Certainly looks like the Lamanov," he said after a moment. "Same size, colour."

"She left Tasiilaq when we did," I pointed out. "And it was her helicopter that came after us."

"How long?" Cheznev said, his voice breaking.

Bridges turned. "What?"

"Before she gets here. How long?"

"Twenty, maybe thirty minutes."

Cheznev paused, looking down at the ice, tears welling in his eyes. Then he raised his head slowly. "Could I have the gun?"

The words came clearly, calmly. He looked from Bridges to me and I realized he wasn't shivering anymore. I saw in his wrinkled face a fearless quality. Determination gleamed in his bloodshot eyes like ship's lights in a dense fog.

"Please," he pleaded. "The gun."

I believe I would have chosen the same fate in his shoes. He was probably convinced that he was going to die anyway.

"Better give it to him," I said.

Bridges shook his head.

"We can't just let him kill himself," he said.

"Don't talk shit. It's his life. Let him end it how he pleases."

"But they may not even kill him."

Cheznev was all of a rage and I didn't blame him.

"Of course they will kill me, you fool," he roared. "The gun, please. It is the only way."

Bridges kept calm and spoke softly, almost as if he were the only sane one among us. "There are bound to be US ships and aircraft in the area. We might still be spotted yet."

"Bollocks," I said. "There's no way that Ruskie ship won't get to us first and you know it."

He turned on me angrily. "He doesn't get the gun and that's final. Now shut up, Preston."

I stood there, shaking. What was I meant to do short of taking the gun from him, in which event he might well deem it his duty to put an end to my insistence once and for all with a sharp crack over the head or even a bullet to the brain.

I looked anxiously at the ship. It was gaining on us now and I could even see the white foam being churned up by the reinforced bow. I wondered why, if she was the Lamanov, the helicopter had not been sent on ahead.

Cheznev began to sob loudly and buried his face in his hands. I ignored him and concentrated on the approaching ship.

She was trying now to manoeuvre between a couple of bergs by following a lead which took her slightly off course. As a result I got a side view of the port bow and the letters painted on it - OSS 01.

For a moment I couldn't believe my eyes and I recited the figures to myself again. Satisfied I wasn't mistaken, I turned to the others.

"We were wrong," I said simply. "She isn't the Lamanov. She just looks the same. This ship has OSS written on the bow."

Bridges was aghast. "That's Oceanographic Survey Ship - American."

"That's why there's been no helicopter," I said. "She hasn't got one."

Bridges started to say something, but the words failed to materialize. Instead he just stared, open mouthed, at the approaching ship.

I turned to Cheznev. He was smiling. "Looks like you're going to be all right," I said. "And you can thank your lucky stars you didn't get that gun."

But then the smile suddenly faded from his face. He stared beyond me, his eyes filled with disbelief.

As I turned I saw the revolver in the CIA man's hand, finger poised on the trigger.

TWENTY THREE

"Move nearer to the hummock where you can't be seen from the ship," Bridges said in a cold, strange voice.

"What the bloody hell…"

He motioned with the gun. "Just move, Preston."

He reached forward, took my arm in a grip that threatened to tear it from the socket and shoved me back towards the mound of ice.

For the moment my mind could not grasp what was happening. My thoughts were a senseless shambles and even the pressure of his hand had been hardly felt.

"Now stay there."

I stood, without moving, looking at Bridges as if it was for the first time. Indeed it was for the first time. This was a different Bridges to the man I had grown to like and respect.

This man was desperate enough to sweat heavily and tremble even though he held the upper hand.

Bridges took the recumbent Cheznev by the hood of his parka, dragged him across the ice to where I was standing, and stepped back, gun in hand.

"I'd hoped it wouldn't come to this," he said.

"To what?" I blurted. "Are you out of your mind?"

"Far from it."

"Then what are you doing, for God's sake?"

"Pointing a gun at you."

"But I do not understand," Cheznev broke in. "The Americans. Your people. They are here. There is no longer any reason why I should die."

"Correction," Bridges said. "The need has just arisen."

"Why don't you explain yourself?" I said.

"Is that really necessary, Preston?"

He fixed me with a stare and it took perhaps five seconds for me to get the message. Even then I couldn't believe it.

He took it for granted that I understood. "So you see, Preston. I can't afford to let them take Cheznev alive — or you now for that matter."

"Tell me what is going on," Cheznev pleaded.

I spat out the words. "Our friend Bridges here is really working for your people. He's the leak I've heard about. Am I right?"

Bridges grinned, those splendid teeth becoming the focal point of his handsome face. "I didn't intend that you should ever know."

"Which is why you didn't want Cheznev to have the gun."

He shrugged. "The Russians want the bastard alive."

Suddenly a lot of things made sense. How the Russians knew Cheznev was intending to defect in the first instance; why the police raid on the house in Reykjavik was foiled; how Sidorov knew the police were taking me to the embassy.

"And I take it you somehow managed to give your friends the location of the berg."

172

"You're guessing good, Preston. But what I forgot to tell them was that I'd be going along myself. Which is why they opened fire from the helicopter."

"How did you let them know from the airfield anyway?" I said.

"A contact in town."

"Gudren!"

"To be honest I didn't think they'd send her," he said. "But I wanted someone to back me up down here if things went wrong. I think they were just keen to get her out of the capital in a hurry."

"So it was you who clobbered me."

He nodded. "The hotel room door was open. I slipped in when you were talking so you didn't hear me."

Bridges lifted the gun.

"So what do you propose to do now?" I said.

"Isn't it obvious."

"Bullets do show up," I said. "You'll never get away with it."

"I've thought about that," he said, as confident as ever. "You see, I intend to say that you, Preston, were really working for the other side all along. You shot Cheznev when you saw the ship was American and I had no choice but to shoot you."

"Very heroic," I said.

"That's just what I think."

"You'll probably get a medal."

He laughed. "If I stop this old goose passing on what he knows they'll owe me a lot more than a medal."

173

"A nice fat bonus in next month's envelope you mean?"

"Something like that."

He glanced again at the ship. "Okay, end of conversation."

"But you can't…" Cheznev began.

"Shut up," Bridges told him.

His hand tightened around the butt of the revolver. I knew my time was up. Hesitate and I was dead. So I lunged forward. The gun blasted and my right shoulder exploded. It was like being hit with a sledgehammer swung by a giant who'd put all his strength behind it.

I threw all my weight into him and grabbed blindly for the gun. It went off a second time, but I didn't feel anything so I assumed the bullet missed.

We went spinning across the ice in a wild embrace. Bridges had one arm around my neck and was trying to work his other hand — the one that held the gun — into a position that would enable him to blast me in the face.

When he realized he was getting nowhere he changed his tactics and rolled over onto his back, dragging me on top of him.

He tried to free his right arm, determined to get a crack at my face, but it didn't work. I pinned his wrist to the ice and started to bend it backwards.

His mistake had been to pull me into him because as a result his movements were restricted. I applied some more pressure on his wrist and he began to moan and curse loudly.

At last he couldn't take the pain any longer and let go of the gun, but he realized my intention and somehow found the strength to heave us both away from it. We rolled over several times and Bridges clambered to his feet.

I grabbed his left ankle, pulled his leg from under him and watched him fall.

Then I tried to roll towards the gun, but the pain in the shoulder that now harboured a bullet brought me up sharp. It was excruciating. For a few seconds I couldn't move, could only lie there wincing, tears streaming down my cheeks as my shoulder throbbed.

Bridges saw his chance and sprang to his feet. He stood over me, staring down, lips tight across his teeth. Then he surprised me by not going for the gun. He grabbed my right wrist and dragged me across the ice.

The cliff edge was only inches away when he let go of my wrist. He walked around me and I realized then his intention. He started kicking me towards the edge.

Then I heard the shot.

The kicking stopped abruptly and for a moment there was complete silence, save for the subdued creaking of the ice beneath us.

I looked up as Bridges began to fall. His face was screwed up in an expression of pain and disbelief. He fell across me. His knees smashed into my thigh and, his stomach landed on the sharp edge of the cliff. Then he slid over.

I crawled to the edge and looked down. He had landed on the platform of ice at the base of the berg — one hundred feet down. He was obviously dead.

I turned over slowly, with difficulty. Cheznev was on his knees, a small stream of smoke rising from the barrel of the revolver held tightly in his good hand.

I smiled faintly and he smiled back, before dropping the gun and sinking to the ice.

EPILOGUE

The drama that unfolded in the Denmark Strait did not get reported. A news blackout was imposed which everyone adhered to. It suited the Americans and the Russians. They didn't want the world to know what had happened.

But the blackout did not extend to Cheznev's defection and the secrets he revealed about Russian policy in the Arctic.

There was a huge diplomatic spat which led the United Nations to organise a series of meetings aimed at avoiding another Cold War.

The Russians found themselves on the back foot. They were embarrassed and apologetic. They tried to say that their strategy for the Arctic region was a work in progress. And that the goals set out in the documents disclosed by Cheznev had not been set in stone.

Of course, nobody believed them.

As for me, well it took several weeks for my wound to heal. I had to rest up in my apartment, which was just as well because I didn't have a plane.

But that was going to be a short-lived situation because the American government had decided to buy me a new one for services rendered. They had also offered to buy one for Bill Osborn, but Bill told them to give him the cash instead, having accepted that his flying days were over. Being a pilot was not compatible with being a drunk.

I heard no more about Sidorov and Gudren or whatever their real names were. I assumed they both eventually ended up back in Moscow or were now making mischief in some other part of the world.

I heard from Cheznev, though. He called me to wish me well and to tell me that he was moving to a home in one of the southern States of North America. Somewhere warm and sunny, he said.

As far away as possible from the chill winds of the Arctic.

THE END

James Raven
By the same author:

Rollover
Urban Myth
Brutal Revenge
Stark Warning

http://www.james-raven.com/

Printed in Great Britain
by Amazon

77268911R00113